PAINTED TRILLIUM

A Novel of the Civil War

Robert Brandt

Wandering in the Words Press

PUBLISHED BY WANDERING IN THE WORDS PRESS

ISBN-10: 0-9967878-5-2
ISBN-13: 978-0-9967878-5-7
First Edition

In memory of my mother,
Edith Davis Brandt

OTHER BOOKS BY ROBERT BRANDT

Natural Nashville: A Guide to the Greenways and Nature Parks

Compass American Guides – Tennessee

Middle Tennessee on Foot: Hikes in the Woods & Walks on Country Roads

Touring the Middle Tennessee Backroads

Tennessee Hiking Guide

Painted trillium. (*Trillium undulatum*). A member of the lily family, one of several spring-blooming trilliums growing wild in the Tennessee woods. Painted trillium is distinguishable from the more common white trillium by the colorful maroon splotches at the base of each petal. Trillium is from the Latin *tri* meaning "three"; the flower's parts occur in threes.

I deem it my duty to repeat to you the great dissatisfaction that is felt here at your inactivity.

General-in-Chief Henry Halleck in Washington
to
Major General William S. Rosecrans at Murfreesboro

PROLOGUE

Carrie Blaylock stood alone in the kitchen of the large house that doubled as her home and her school. Her sky blue dress slid into a heap around her ankles. Her chemise came off next. She tossed it into the hamper with the dress. Her drawers were last. She tugged the draw string open and stepped out of them one foot at a time. With her eyes shut, she ran the tips of her fingers across the dusting of freckles on her cheeks, down her thin neck and girlish breasts, and along her narrow hips. She shivered from the chill it brought.

She dipped her hands into the pot of warm water on the stove. With the lathered washcloth, she took away the soot and dust from her trip. After she rinsed, she tingled as the fluffy towel worked its way back and forth over her skin. She poked her head through the neck of a clean nightgown and let it fall around her.

After shutting off the gas lights in the kitchen, she climbed the stairs back to her second-floor bedroom.

Carrie felt warm and clean, letting down her hair at the dressing table. Her turquoise eyes stared back at her in the mirror, and she leaned in for a closer look. It confirmed what she'd seen in her reflection in the window of the railroad car: a few streaks of gray in her sandy hair.

She slid under the down quilt on her four-poster bed and reached for the Bible on her nightstand.

It was still early, barely past sundown on Easter Sunday 1884.

***

The day before, she and Sam had boarded the morning train for an overnight visit to the farm where Carrie had grown up. No matter how many times she returned, she couldn't shake the tug of apprehension as Murfreesboro drew near. No one but her knew for sure what had happened back in the spring of 1863, but some still harbored suspicions. Encountering one of them might provoke a scene. Her anxiety blew away like a wispy puff of cloud at the sight of her brother-in-law waiting at the station; he was the only person she recognized.

"There's Henry," blurted Carrie, more like one of her schoolgirls than the staid headmistress of forty-two years.

Carrie and Sam rose in unison when the train halted, only to be thrust back onto the hard seat when the cars lurched forward before stopping again. They exchanged startled looks, and then quickly broke out laughing. Sam yanked their bags off the overhead rack and followed as Carrie accepted the hand of the black porter standing straight as a tulip poplar in his crisp, navy blue uniform and starched, white shirt.

"It's so good to see you," said Carrie, planting a quick kiss on her sister's husband's cheek.

"You're as lovely as ever, Sister." Henry wrapped his left arm around her.

"Oh Henry, I'm just a drab old school-marm."

"A school-marm, but never drab. What about it, Major?" Henry replied, extending his right hand.

"You'll not get an argument out of me," Sam shot back, shaking Henry's hand and casting a warm glance in Carrie's direction.

Henry's two-horse carriage was tethered on the opposite side of the station house, and when the three of them reached it, Sam helped Carrie into the front seat, tossed their bags onto the rear seat, and hopped in beside them.

"Say, I've an idea," Henry said, prodding the horses. "Let's take a drive around the Square and out East Main Street. There's new construction I'm eager to show you."

"Let me guess; you sold the lumber," Sam said.

Henry smiled and glanced over his shoulder. "I always knew you Yankee boys were clever."

"A banker always likes to see economic activity," Sam said. "What about you, my dear?"

"You two go on after you drop me off. I do want to head straight home." It had been two decades since she'd moved to Nashville, but Carrie still called River Bluff Farm home.

Henry pulled away from the station and guided his mares out the Salem Pike. "These trees, it seems like they've grown another foot every time I visit," Carrie said to no one in particular. She studied the passing oaks, hickories, and sugar maples lining the road. Inhaling a deep breath of fresh country air, she recalled the time she'd feared that this verdant landscape was lost forever.

The lane into the farm penetrated one of the ubiquitous cedar thickets that dot this part of Middle Tennessee and then made a right turn to split the orchard. Carrie's heart raced at her first glimpse of the two-story, white-framed house standing atop the slight rise beyond the pear, peach, and cherry trees.

"They're here!" they heard the youngest child cry as Henry pulled to the head of the circle and set the brake. Whenever they visited, Sam stuffed his coat pockets with hard candy. David and Louise, in their teens now, hesitated for an instant as if they'd outgrown it, and then joined their younger brother rifling through the pockets of Sam's suit coat.

Carrie watched the melee with delight until her niece and nephews were satisfied they'd uncovered every last piece, and then she accepted Sam's hand and stepped down to the crunch of her high-top shoes on brown creek pebbles. David and Louise lugged the bags off the carriage while Sam joined Henry in the front seat.

"We should be back in an hour, hour-and-a-half at the latest," Henry shouted behind them as they rounded the circle headed back through the orchard.

"Be careful boys," called Carrie, betraying a deeply embedded fear that she may never again see them alive.

Watching the carriage disappear into the cedars, she recalled the first time she'd brought Sam home with her and how he and Henry had hit it off right from the start. Carrie had remarked to her sister then how strange it seemed that the men who'd actually fought each other got on so well while those who'd stayed home remained so bitter even after all these years. It was mostly the women who wouldn't give it up. The war had made widows out of many and bound countless others to spinsterhood. They reserved their fiercest anger for any of their number whom they suspected of not fully embracing the cause, their glorious Lost Cause.

Louise dragged Carrie's bag into the house and up to the room that was once Carrie's. Carrie looked forward to her nights alone there with her niece and had thought more than once that if she'd been blessed with children, she'd want a daughter just like her.

The boy hauled Sam's bag to the extra bedroom.

Standing in the stillness, Carrie studied the changes her sister and her husband had made since Sarah inherited the house and thirty-two acres from their mother. They'd replaced the one-story Greek Revival portico with a broad front porch across the length of the house, knocked down the old kitchen on the back, and built in its place a two-story "L." It held the new kitchen downstairs, and upstairs the extra bedroom. That's where Sam slept when they visited.

A peculiar sensation suddenly seized Carrie. It was as if she were viewing a painting instead of the real house. Her mind traveled back to the first time she experienced the oddity of sensing that a place was familiar and unfamiliar at the same time. It was during the war on a visit to Nashville. She knew the landmarks from her four years at the Nashville

Female Academy, yet it felt like she'd never been there before.

***

"What can I do?" Carrie asked, walking into the kitchen and exchanging hugs with her sister. For as long as anyone could remember, the Blaylocks' custom was to serve Easter dinner on Saturday.

"I've saved the bread for you," Sarah said. Carrie's love for baking was well-known in the family.

Once Carrie had prepared the dough and placed it in the oven, she joined Sarah at the table for some catching up, "making up for lost time" the sisters liked to call it. Because of their difference in ages—Carrie was six years older—they hadn't been particularly close growing up. In some ways they'd become more so as adults. Yet in some ways they hadn't. Sarah always seemed eager to hear the latest news from Carrie's school, but Carrie often felt a trace of unease sharing it, fearful that she'd come across as haughty, like the life she'd chosen was superior to the one her little sister had chosen.

"I've already turned away a few girls for next year's class," Carrie explained. "Many parents now want their daughters to be trained in something more than being a wife and mother. I know I would."

Sarah laughed. "It's not all that bad."

"Oh Sister, I didn't mean anything by that. You're a wonderful mother." Carrie shifted in her chair and told Sarah that another of her girls who would be enrolling in Vassar College in the fall wouldn't be required to spend a year in the preparatory department.

"My, that certainly speaks well of you," Sarah said.

"Perhaps. I believe she's the first Southern girl to go straight into the college, if you don't count the ones from Baltimore and Washington."

"Carrie, I'll share with you something I haven't even shared with Henry." Sarah leaned in and lowered her voice. "I've thought about that for Louise."

"College?"

"Maybe, but at least have her study with you."

"She's such a bright girl."

"I assume she can board with you during the week?"

Carrie felt the grip of panic for a split second and hoped Sarah would attribute the rise of red on her face to the warm kitchen. "Of course." Carrie shifted again in her chair. "You've heard of the McGavocks?"

"Sure."

Carrie related that one of them had a daughter graduating from a new college up in Massachusetts called Smith, and the girl's father had been to see Carrie to say that his daughter was eager to come back south and help educate girls. Carrie was considering expanding the school and offering her a position.

"Do you have the money for it?" Sarah asked.

"I'll have to borrow it. Sam and I've discussed it. My biggest fear is that if there is another panic or yellow fever outbreak, then parents wouldn't be able to afford it."

"And if you couldn't repay the bank, then Mother's money and all you've worked for would be lost."

"Yes, Mother's money," Carrie said quietly.

As a girl, she hadn't thought it out of the ordinary for a minister's family to be living in a substantial house on thirty-two acres. As she got older, though, she heard talk. Other children passed on what they overheard from their parents. "Those Blaylocks must have money coming in from somewhere." It wasn't until their mother died that Carrie learned just how well off her mother was.

Amanda LaBruce Blaylock came from a wealthy family of Philadelphia merchants and migrated to Middle Tennessee in the 1850s when her husband, the Rev. David Blaylock, answered the call to launch an Episcopal church in Murfreesboro. With the clouds of sectional crisis darkening, her brother convinced them that the bulk of Amanda's assets would be safer back east. In her will, Amanda left the house and farm to her married daughter and left her cash and railroad bonds to Carrie.

Carrie found her eyes drooping shut in the warmth of the kitchen. She'd stayed up late. It was her practice every Good Friday to compose long letters to two women she didn't see much of anymore but whom she still thought of as her closest friends, Lizzy Schultz in Cincinnati and her sister-in-law, Martha Davenport, in Texas.

"Do you mind if I go up and lie down?"

"Mind? Why would I mind?"

"The bread will have to come out."

"Will you ever stop being so hard on yourself?"

It was a familiar refrain. So was Carrie's response. She said nothing.

"Go upstairs and rest, Sister. I will take care of the bread."

***

Carrie leaned against the closed bedroom door. She tried to visualize the room when it was hers, and that one day in particular, but she couldn't. It was as if it had happened in some far, distant place.

This was one star in the constellation of bittersweet thoughts and feelings that had become habitual on her visits home: apprehension returning to Murfreesboro, sadness upon leaving, and though she thought poorly of herself for it, envy of her younger sister. Men stopped and stared at Sarah; that's how beautiful she was. She had a sober, faithful husband and three well-behaved, inquisitive children.

The sisters were "as different as night and day" their mother used to tell them. A person had to study to detect a resemblance. Sarah had their mother's creamy brown skin, alluring dark eyes, and hair the color of a buckeye. Now in her mid-thirties, she was blessed with the same hour-glass figure she had on her wedding day. Carrie was a bit taller and more slender. Her hair was a wheat-like color she'd always branded as boring, and a few girlhood freckles lingered on the tops of her cheeks.

Carrie had always been calm, deliberate, and purposeful. As a girl, Sarah was passionate and impulsive. Carrie loved to read and study so much that the other girls labeled her bookish, while Sarah craved socializing. Parties and boys interested her more.

The war, with all its cruelty and deprivation, taught the sisters different lessons. Being without a man to protect her and to provide for her were calamities Sarah vowed to avoid, and she'd set her sights on Henry Frierson the day he arrived from Columbia to help his uncle run the lumber yard. Sarah became a bride in her nineteenth year and a mother in her twentieth.

Carrie, though, learned the opposite. She would make her own way. She would never be dependent on any man.

***

The sound of Henry and Sam returning from their jaunt stirred Carrie from her nap, and after smoothing the full skirt of her dress, she went downstairs to retrieve her cape for the ritual visit to the cemetery. Sam offered to take her in Henry's two-seat buggy, but she declined. She wanted to make the trip alone. And she wanted to walk, to fill her senses with the comforting sights, sounds, and smells of the season. The pink and white blossoms of the fruit trees quaking in the soft breeze buzzed with the frenetic coming and going of honeybees, and a squawking mockingbird let Carrie know she was unhappy with an intruder near her nest.

It took Carrie about half an hour along the path next to the pike to reach the Courthouse Square. She stopped and stood as inconspicuously as she could with her back against a building. Finally, she thought, some prosperity is returning. The Courthouse had been restored to its original grandeur, and new buildings were going up. The Square was filled this Saturday before Easter with country folks carrying tote bags and gaggles of town girls peering into store windows. Men and women lounged on the benches in front of the Courthouse while children played on the green lawn. After lingering for a minute, Carrie walked on to the cemetery.

It had changed since her last visit. A waist-high, hoop and dart wrought-iron fence enclosed the graveyard, and a graceful arch rose over the entrance. Walking past the mass grave of Confederate soldiers, Carrie speculated as she always did how many of their families ever knew what had become of them. The Federals had buried the dead on the Stones River battlefield, and after the war, the remains, or what was left of them, were dug up and reburied here.

Carrie thought about approaching one of the several knots of people she saw standing around graves but decided to keep to herself. With her covered head down, she picked her way past markers and monuments in all shapes and sizes until she reached two headstones beneath a tall conical cedar.

"Rev. David C. Blaylock, 1814-1861. Amanda L. Blaylock, 1816-1872." Carrie had cut some daffodils and red tulips from the side of the house, and she knelt to lay half of them in front of the headstone. She allowed her eyes to drop shut and her mind to fill with a vision she often had: her parents strolling hand-in-hand across a shimmering, emerald field bordered by deep green cedars.

Carrie stepped to the next headstone. "Travis D. Blaylock, 1838-1862." She knelt and placed the remaining flowers. Her thoughts went to her brother's wife, Martha, who'd remained Carrie's steadfast friend and confidant through it all. The family had no complaints about the man from Texas Martha had married after the war. He was so considerate that he actually sought Amanda's permission to marry her dead son's widow.

***

On Sundays it was Henry's custom to cook a big breakfast, so the next day they all sat down to platters of pork loin, biscuits, gravy, and eggs the children had gathered on Saturday. Sarah opened a jar of peach preserves put up the summer before.

"I'll clean up. You folks go on," said Carrie as the church hour approached. She didn't like missing the Easter service at the very church her father had founded back in the fifties, but she'd resolved to never again subject herself to the cold looks of women she'd once counted as her friends.

After finishing in the kitchen, Carrie and Sam took advantage of the solitude and the robin's-egg-blue sky to wander out to the gazebo on the bluff above the Stones River. The eight-sided structure had been restored since she moved away and was on this day surrounded by a blaze of blooming redbuds. Sam went straight for the bench inside it, but Carrie took a few more steps to the crest of the bluff jutting ten feet above the river, swollen by runoff from the early spring rains.

Peering down into the river, Carrie spotted a shiny dark stick trapped in an eddy, endlessly circling round and round. Like my memory of that spring, she thought. It never leaves. She lost herself in the sight and sound of the river, and for a second when she snapped out of it, didn't remember where she was, which frightened her a little.

Turning away from the river, she saw Sam sitting ramrod straight with his alert eyes fixed on her. Her eyes never left his as she walked to the bench and took her seat next to him. She was conscious of the sounds—the river lapping against the bluff, the cry of a pileated woodpecker floating through the tree canopy, the shrill call of a red-tailed hawk soaring above, and the rustle of the forest's new growth quaking in the slight breath of wind.

Here at her favorite place on earth, Carrie felt safe from prying eyes. Here at this serene spot she didn't have to worry about her risky life. Sam's long arm drew her snug against his shoulder. She felt protected and secure.

***

"Leave, dutiful Sister, leave. You'll miss your train." Sarah took the dishtowel from Carrie and pushed her toward the front of the house.

"It's been wonderful," said Carrie, kissing her sister on the cheek and doing the same to Louise. "Goodbye, my special niece. Will you come to Nashville for a visit when school's out?"

"If Mama will let me," said Louise with a hopeful glance at her mother.

"We'll see," Sarah said.

The train from Chattanooga was already at the station when they arrived. With the conductor bellowing "all aboard," Carrie gave her brother-in-law a hug and climbed the narrow steps onto the open platform at the end of the car. Sam followed with their bags.

***

The train thumped across the short bridge spanning Stewart Creek, and Carrie gazed out at the pale green willows illuminated by the afternoon's golden sun. She saw in her reflection the tears gathering in her eyes. She couldn't have known it back then, but it was here at this very spot, twenty-one-years earlier, that her life was altered forever. Sam didn't stir when she turned away from the window and rested her hand on his.

Was he asleep or only pretending? She was never sure. He always seemed to nod off the instant the train rattled over the Stones River. This way he wouldn't have to see the killing fields and the rows of bone-white headstones lining the green space between the tracks and the Nashville Pike. And this way she could have her private moment of grief.

Carrie knew that by the time the chain of drafty cars jerked to a stop at the Nashville depot, she'd again be her normal self. She'd walk back into living her dream as headmistress of her own school, but even in her wildest fantasies she couldn't have imagined her life with Sam.

***

Sarah and her daughter were alone in the kitchen putting away the last evidence of another happy Easter when Louise turned to her mother. "Mama, I don't understand about Aunt Carrie and Uncle Sam."

"Don't understand what, dear?"

"They don't sleep … I mean, ah … when they're here … ah, what I mean is, they're not like you and Papa."

Sarah froze at first and then turned to look directly into the eyes of her daughter. "They're not married."

"Why?"

"I'm not entirely sure, darling."

"But you're sisters. You talk."

"Even sisters don't share everything. I know she wants to keep her school."

"Can't she keep her school if she's married?"

"You'd think so, Louise, but there are some things a married woman can't do like an unmarried woman can. And …" Sarah stopped to collect her thoughts.

"And what, Mama?"

It's only natural for a girl blossoming into a woman to be curious about these things, thought Sarah. I was about the same age as Louise when it happened. "Let's finish up here, and we'll talk about it later, at bedtime."

***

Carrie and Sam climbed up Church Street out of Nashville's railroad gulch and came to the corner of Spruce Street. She paused for a look at the State Capitol high on the hill. She'd always admired the building. It was brightened now by the clear day's last rays of sun illuminating the Stars and Stripes fluttering atop it, like the willows she saw from the train.

They walked south on Spruce Street to the substantial Italianate-style red brick house taking up the corner at the Cumberland Alley. "MISS BLAYLOCK'S SCHOOL FOR GIRLS" read the sign above the door. Sam unlocked it, walked in first, set down the bags, and lit some gas lamps while Carrie hung her cape on the hall rack. In the kitchen, she drew water into a pot and set it on a lit burner. Sam had her bag upstairs and her bedroom lamps lit by the time she got there.

He gently pulled her to him, took her head in his hands, and softly kissed her forehead. No words passed as he turned and went back down the stairs. Gathering his bag, he let himself out and locked the front door behind him.

***

I would have been a good father. The joy Sam felt horsing around with Sarah and Henry's children was fresh in his mind as he finished his journal entry for Easter Sunday, 1884. Alone in his rooms above the Commerce Bank where he was in his seventh year as a vice president, Sam repeated out loud the same prayer he said every night: "Thank you, God, for bringing me to her."

He slipped off his boots, set them alongside his chair, removed the suit he'd worn to Murfreesboro, and hung it in the closet. He stepped into an old pair of work pants with suspenders and then slipped into a scruffy coat. He laced up the brogans he picked off the closet floor, retrieved his old slouch hat, and pulled it down close to his eyes. Out on the street he didn't look much different from the stevedores working the Cumberland River waterfront just to the east.

Sam made his way down the steep hill on High Street away from the Capitol and turned west up the narrow Cumberland Alley. He stopped for a look in all directions. Satisfied no one was watching him, he fished out the key he kept in the pocket of his old pants and let himself in the back door of Miss Blaylock's School for Girls.

***

Louise was still enough of a little girl to want her mother to rub her back before she drifted off to sleep. These opportunities wouldn't last much longer, and Sarah cherished every one. They were silent in the darkness before the girl spoke.

"What else were you going to tell me about Aunt Carrie and Uncle Sam?"

"They both seem happy."

"I can tell how much she likes him."

"I'm thankful she has someone now. She was alone for so long."

"Aunt Carrie doesn't have any friends around here. Is that why she moved to Nashville?"

Sarah turned away for a few seconds. "There's more to it."

"Is that when she started her school?"

"She taught first at another school and had a little room there. Sometime in the seventies, a man from up North, a Mr. Peabody, started a college for teachers, and your aunt was in the first class. About the time she finished, Mother passed, and with the money she inherited, Carrie started her own school."

"Doesn't she want to be a mother?"

"All women want to be mothers, Louise, but sometimes God has other plans."

"Why doesn't she marry Sam?"

"As I said, she'd probably have to give up her school if she married, and … "

"And what?"

"Something happened in your Aunt Carrie's life a long time ago."

"Do you know what it was?"

"We were all living here then."

"Will you tell me about it?"

Sarah thought for a second. She'd have to carefully choose her words.

"It was during the war."

CHAPTER ONE

January 1863

First Lieutenant Jean Troussant worked to keep his focus on the girl. This way he might avoid succumbing to the misery and despair sweeping through the army as it slogged along the muddy road churned by thousands of feet and hooves. The boys believed they were on the verge of a victory. Yet just as he'd done in Kentucky in the fall when whipping the Yankees seemed to be within their grasp, General Braxton Bragg ordered a retreat.

The soldiers' anger and confusion was compounded by their complete lack of knowledge of where they were headed. They were trudging southbound through the sleet on the Shelbyville Pike; that's all they knew. And to add to their humiliation, they were leaving behind at Murfreesboro hundreds of wounded comrades for the Yankees to deal with as they pleased. Even one of Bragg's subordinate generals spoke out: "All our hard fighting thrown away, as usual."

Now and then, Lieutenant Troussant saw groups of men disappear from the quagmire into the darkness. He knew who they were and where they were going; Middle Tennessee boys headed home, walking away from the war now that there wouldn't be an army around to protect their homes and their families. "I'll tell you straight out," a sergeant told him as his men drifted out of the ranks. "I ain't up to keep on fightin' just for them cotton planters, them that started this whole mess in the first place."

On this retreat, though, the young lieutenant at least had something to keep him going, a cause he didn't have on the cold, hungry march out of Kentucky. During the army's six-week stay at Murfreesboro, he'd made the acquaintance of a girl; more than an acquaintance, truth be told. The lieutenant vowed that wherever he was when the war ended, no matter how far away he was, and even before going home to New Orleans, he'd return to Tennessee. He'd find the girl.

***

"Eleven!" Carrie Blaylock observed the fuzzy image of the ticking clock resting atop her dressing table. "I've been asleep more than twelve hours!"

She threw back the cover, rolled out of bed, and slipped on her snug, rabbit-hide house shoes. She didn't change out of her nightgown. She didn't need to. She'd slept in the same blood-splattered homespun dress she'd been wearing for days. Her last conscious act had been to slide under the thick comforter. Three days and nights of hardly any sleep finally caught up with her.

Carrie scurried down the stairs to find her mother alone in the parlor comforted by a warm fire.

"Mother, please forgive me for not being up to fix breakfast." Carrie took a seat next to her mother on the settee.

"It's been difficult for all of us."

The two of them sat quietly for a moment before Carrie broke the silence. "I have a sense that something happened during the night. I was awakened by a sound I couldn't make out. I thought it was just more sleet, but now I'm not sure."

Amanda Blaylock turned and stared wearily into the fire.

"Mother, did you hear something during the night?"

"I heard it," said her mother in a hushed tone with her blank gaze fixed on the fire.

"Do you have any idea what it was?"

"I do now," Amanda said.

"Well?"

"It was the sound of an army retreating."

"You mean Rosecrans took the Yankees back to Nashville?"

"No."

"For heaven's sake, Mother, tell me what it was then."

"It was the Confederate army retreating."

"The Confederate army? That can't be true."

"See for yourself."

Carrie looked out the front window. The Louisiana artillery that had been camped in the orchard was gone. Its only evidence was steamy smoke rising from the remains of campfires.

"Bragg made his men leave Murfreesboro in that dark, freezing rain? He must be mad," Carrie said.

"There is certainly no shortage of those who believe that." Amanda Blaylock looked back at her oldest daughter. "But apparently Jefferson Davis isn't one of them. He heard the complaints, made his long trip here from Richmond last month, but left things just as they were. Oh, there was a grand review, the sumptuous dinner at the Maneys' and all that silliness, but anyone with any sense could tell that something's rotten in the army. I'm coming around to thinking Davis is the biggest fool of them all."

They sat in silence absorbing the full implication of what had happened. There would be yet another Federal occupation. Only this time it would be by an entire army. And this time, the Yankees might be here for good.

***

When Major General William S. Rosecrans satisfied himself that the enemy had fled, his battered boys in blue stumbled into Murfreesboro on January 5, 1863, and established camps in and around the town of about 4,000. Rosecrans judged that his 45,000 men had neither the energy nor the material to press further, not just now. The toll from the Battle of Stones River was ghastly: 24,645 casualties, nearly one-third of both armies. The mercurial Ohioan set about re-supplying his wounded army with men, food, clothing, weapons, ammunition, horses and mules for the next push south. That would come in the spring, maybe as early as March, most likely in April, certainly no later than the first week in May.

To accomplish his massive build-up, the Union general needed the rail link connecting his army to Nashville and points north. So he directed construction crews to restore the thirty-five miles of wrecked rail between Murfreesboro and Nashville. By February, the line was open.

CHAPTER TWO

February 1863

It was over as quickly as it had begun. The cracks of gunfire faded, the train lurched forward, and a pair of unseen hands under Carrie's shoulders lifted her back onto the hard bench. When she'd been stuffed onto the grimy floor of the freezing train car moments before, her mother's warning had reverberated in her head: *You'll be risking your life, but I can't stop you. You're a grown woman now.*

Carrie instinctively jerked off a glove and raised her trembling hand to her left cheek. It brought a trace of blood.

"It doesn't look too bad, just a scrape." The man offered her a handkerchief.

Pressing it to her cheek, she turned to see his face for the first time.

"Charles Bradley, miss. Sorry to have shoved you to the floor, but you could've been hit."

As soon as she'd taken her seat in the ramshackle car, Carrie had buried her head in a book, intent on staying like that all the way to Nashville. His blue pants and muddy boots were all she'd seen of her seatmate until now. The man had a boyish, almost delicate look, and if it weren't for some gray streaks in his close-cropped beard he could have passed for someone her age.

She observed on his shoulder the single star of a brigadier general. "I'm grateful for your concern, General."

"You must have urgent business in Nashville."

Trying to get away from this miserable war, she thought. "A visit with friends."

As the young general studied her face, another of her mother's admonitions flashed through Carrie's mind: *Men will get ideas. Ladies don't travel alone.*

"I take it you're loyal to be able to make this trip," the general said.

Carrie felt a rush of panic. She was not a good liar. But if she responded with the truth, this seemingly kind man might have her thrown off the train to mercies of the Yankee deserters, bushwhackers, and runaway slaves roaming the wasted countryside. So she flatly repeated the line she'd been rehearsing. "I've signed the oath."

The oath of loyalty to the United States was becoming a powerful weapon in the Union army's arsenal. Those who refused to sign it were subject to being locked up or exiled outside the lines. When the Federals took over the first time, early in 1862, the Blaylocks were the first in the county to sign the oath, and now that the Yankees were again in control, Carrie was careful always to carry her copy.

> *I do solemnly swear (or affirm) that I will support, protect and defend the Constitution and Government of the United States against all enemies, whether domestic or foreign, and that I will bear true faith, allegiance and loyalty to the same, any ordinance, resolution or law of any State, convention or legislature to the contrary notwithstanding; and further, that I do this with full determination, pledge and purpose, without any mental reservation whatsoever: So help me God.*
>
> *Signed: Carrie Blaylock*

Carrie stiffened to fortify her resolve not to make conversation with this enemy officer. But her interest in who attacked the train prompted her to let down her guard. "Was that Confederate cavalry?"

"Rebel cavalry isn't usually up this far since the battle—bushwhackers I'd say."

Well that's at least one benefit of having our town overrun by an entire army, Carrie thought. They may tear down our fences, raid our smokehouses, and steal our stock, but they do protect us from being robbed at gunpoint—and for women and girls, something even worse.

"How are you fairing in this mess?" the brigadier asked softly.

"We're making out." Carrie worked to keep her face from showing anger. "Come to think of it, your boys did steal our pigs."

"My boys?"

"Federal soldiers."

"How do you know it was soldiers who stole the pigs and not someone else, maybe some darkies on the run?"

"Because I saw them. I begged them not to, but it didn't do any good."

"Do you have any idea who they were?"

Whether the general was really interested or just humoring her, she couldn't tell.

"They talked like they're from around here."

"From Kentucky probably. These things happen when you cluster 50,000 men in one place on a diet of bug-infested hard biscuits and rotten bacon."

"I suppose." Carrie strained to reach her book that had fallen to the floor.

General Bradley picked it up and handed it to her. "What are you reading, if I might ask?"

"Dickens."

"I've read *Great Expectations* and *David Copperfield.* Someday if this war ever ends, I'll read more Dickens."

She found herself smiling, ever so slightly. "I'm hoping to bring books back from Nashville."

"Have you a family?"

"My mother, my younger sister, and me. Mother's a widow." She knew better than to tell him about her brother, Travis, having been in the Confederate army. "And you, sir?"

"I have a wife. That's where I'm going, home on a furlough. We have two boys, ages eleven and nine, and a little girl, five. "

"Where's home?"

"Ohio, Sandusky, up on Lake Erie, a long way from here."

"How long do you have?"

"Only two weeks."

"I'm sure they'll be glad to see you. Where were you posted before the war?"

"I'm a volunteer. Never had a day's military training before the war. I was recently promoted to general officer and given a newly created brigade."

A political general, thought Carrie. A bungling political general had cost her brother his life, the general's life, too, for that matter. But this man didn't strike her as a bungler. And from what she'd heard of Major General William S. Rosecrans, the Army of the Cumberland's commander, he wouldn't recommend for promotion any officer who hadn't served ably.

"What's your civilian occupation back … where did you say?"

"Sandusky, Ohio. A banker. And your family?"

"My father was a minister of the Protestant Episcopal Church and a part-time farmer, a gentleman farmer I guess you'd say."

"Murfreesboro is a firmly secesh town. How does a loyal family get by?"

Her family wasn't "loyal" the way the general meant it. Signing the loyalty oath was a means of survival. She dodged the question. "What else do you like to read, General?"

As the train swayed toward Nashville, they chatted mostly about books, but shared a little about themselves, as well. She enjoyed the diversion, which surprised her. On the surface at least, she'd accepted the prevailing notion among her friends that these villainous invaders were to be avoided at all cost. Deep in her heart, though, she knew better. Her family came from the North, and she'd been born in Philadelphia.

Carrie told the youthful general about the family she was visiting in Nashville. She'd boarded with the Forbeses while a student at the Nashville Female Academy, and her classmate Elizabeth Forbes became her closest friend. Dr. Forbes was originally from Scotland, a physician who'd accepted an invitation to relocate from New York to join the medical faculty at the University of Nashville. He was Unionist in his sympathies, and though she couldn't tell the general, he'd used his connections to arrange the pass Carrie needed for her travel.

The general stood and looked down at her. "You'll have to excuse me, ma'am, I need to have a word with the captain of the guard."

It was only after the general left that Carrie noticed the others in the car. She was the only female as far as she could tell. Some of the men's limbs were nothing more than bloody, bandage-covered stumps. The jaws of some seemed to be held in place only by the filthy rags wrapped around their heads. A few had only one eye with a bloody socket where the other should have been. Most of the men were wrapped in blood-encrusted blankets, and a few of them looked as young as her little sister, Sarah.

Her mind went to her friends in the reading circle who'd delight in seeing such miserable creatures. The worse these enemy soldiers suffered the better. But to Carrie they didn't appear any different from the boys she'd nursed after the battle—just different colored uniforms.

Carrie reached behind her head with both hands and pulled her bonnet forward until the brim was just above her eyes. The big sunbonnet was out of place, but it hid her face. She opened the book on her lap and looked down. But she just stared at it.

Her only certainty in the second year of the war was uncertainty, the taunting uneasiness that comes from never knowing what to expect from one minute to the next. The markers that guided her life had gone missing; the features of the landscape that shaped her identity had mostly vanished. Her expectations for life slowly disappeared over the war-torn horizon, and as they did, a radical self-image incubated in her mind. But it was a hazy image, and the vagueness of it only heightened her apprehension.

A change in surroundings might help. Being somewhere else, even for a short time, might abate her ever-present anxiety. It might offer enough separation from her day-to-day existence to allow her to perceive a path to the new life that would substitute for the life she could no longer count on. Hopefully this trip would do her some good, help her sort things out.

The train chugged onto a side track around Antioch and idled for what seemed like forever until a southbound train crammed with soldiers crept past on the main track.

Taking whole men south and returning broken ones north, she thought. Father was right; no good has come of secession.

The general never returned.

***

Nashville was so transformed by a year of Union army occupation that Carrie hardly recognized it. Seas of stumps covered the graceful hillsides that once held stately stands of oak and sugar maple, and the hilltops were topped by fortifications with cannon protruding from them. A new rail yard west of the depot held at least a dozen locomotives. Everywhere she looked there were tents, and soldiers—soldiers everywhere.

Tennessee's capital city was home to about 17,000 inhabitants before the war, but had swollen to more than 100,000—at least that was the rumor. In addition to soldiers,

Nashville was flooded with civilians working for the government, peddlers and merchants, and runaway slaves, as well as an ample assortment of robbers, pickpockets, and prostitutes.

"You're getting off first, lady." The sergeant's gruff tone was quite a contrast to her seatmate's and caused a slight ripple of fear to rise in her. She wondered if she'd be subjected to this type of behavior on her visit. Carrie tugged her carpetbag from under the seat, slid her book into it, and walked as fast as she could to the open platform at the end of the car. Gathering the skirt of her heavy wool dress with her free hand, she stepped down gingerly.

The instant her feet touched ground she felt a sting in her nose and a burn in her eyes. It's the air, she realized, rancid from the coal smoke entrapping the city.

***

The Forbeses had no way of knowing what time of the day she would reach Nashville, or even what day, for that matter. There was no such thing as planning a trip these days. With no one there to greet her, Carrie lowered her head and struck out on a route she knew well. She'd follow Church Street out of the railroad gulch east toward the Cumberland River until she reached Cherry Street and then walk north to the Forbeses' house.

She hadn't taken more than a few steps before a man trotted in front of her and blocked her path. When she stepped to her left to avoid him, he stepped in front of her. She stepped to her right, and he did too. Carrie raised her head only enough to observe below the brim of her sunbonnet the gold bar of a second lieutenant on the shoulder of his clean blue coat. She couldn't remember seeing a soldier of either army looking so fresh.

"Excuse me, but I'm trying to walk up Church Street," she said with a slight edge to her voice.

"That won't be possible."

"Not possible? What do you mean?"

"No civilian can leave the depot area without a proper pass."

Keeping her head down, she pulled from her pocket the slip of paper the provost marshal in Murfreesboro had given her.

"This is only a pass to get you in and out of our lines around Murfreesboro."

"What?" she asked, raising her head to look the young man in the eye.

"This pass only enables you to get in and out of Murfreesboro."

She snatched it from him.

> *HEADQUARTERS, DEPARTMENT OF THE CUMBERLAND MILITARY PASS*
> *Murfreesboro, Tenn.* Feb 16, 1863
> *GUARDS AND PICKETS*
> *Pass* Carrie Blaylock *out of Murfreesboro* to travel by the cars to Nashville and return by March 14, 1863.
> *By command of Genl. Rosecrans*
> *Maj. William M Wiles, Provost Marshal*
> *By* Capt. Robert M. Goodman, Asst. Provost Marshal

"The provost marshal in Murfreesboro assured me this is the pass I needed to come to Nashville."

"This is insufficient to allow you to travel *in* Nashville."

"What do you mean?"

"To enter Nashville and travel about, you'll need a pass from the provost marshal here."

"Where's the office?"

"I can't let you leave the depot area."

"What am I to do?" Her voice was starting to shake.

"Get on the next train back to Murfreesboro would be my advice."

"After I've gone to all this trouble?"

"Orders are orders, ma'am."

"How long will I have to wait?"

"I guess you've figured out by now that the trains don't run on no set schedule. The line's been reopened only a few weeks. But I'd say two hours or so." The boy glanced toward the crowd of Negro women milling around between them and the depot, and when he turned back to face Carrie, his tone became friendlier. "If you'll go past where them colored women's selling food, there's a bench where you can set. I don't think anyone'll bother you there, but these days you never know. I'll keep an eye out for you."

The instant he said that, the lieutenant snapped his feet together and raised his right hand in a salute.

"As you were."

Carrie recognized the voice. "Oh, General Bradley. The lieutenant here insists this pass is insufficient to allow me to travel in Nashville. He tells me to board the next train back to Murfreesboro."

"General, sir, I am enforcing the …"

"That's not a problem, Lieutenant."

The young general turned to Carrie. "Even general officers are required to have passes these days. If you'll accompany me to the provost marshal's office, we'll see what we can arrange."

"General, sir, my orders are to prohibit any civilian from leaving the depot area without a proper pass," said the lieutenant, his demeanor betraying his humiliation.

"I'm acquainted with the lady, and I can vouch that she's not here to make mischief. If anyone asks, you tell them that Brigadier General Charles Bradley of Negley's Division in General Thomas's Corps overruled you."

"Thank you, sir," said the lieutenant, obviously relieved.

The general took Carrie's bag. They hadn't gone more than a few steps when the lieutenant called out.

"General?"

They stopped and looked back. "What is it, Lieutenant?"

"I'm happy to offer my services to the lady during her stay in Nashville, if she's able to stay."

"She can speak for herself," said the general, looking at Carrie.

What "services," Carrie wondered. She couldn't conceive of any. But she didn't want to hurt the boy's feelings. And who knows, maybe he will come in handy, she thought, recalling the harsh way the sergeant spoke to her on the train. "Thank you, Lieutenant, that's kind of you."

"The name's Howard Geiger of the provost marshal's guard, formerly with the Ninth Indiana."

"Ninth Indiana?" the general said. "In Hazen's Brigade?"

"Correct, sir."

"They took it badly at Stones River."

"Yes, I know."

"You should be grateful you were reassigned."

"Begging your pardon, sir, but I don't see it that way. I should have been there with the others. Before the army marched out of here at Christmas, they asked for sergeants and junior officers who are … who can read and write for assignment to the provost marshal's guard here in Nashville. I was a sergeant, I've had a fair bit of schooling, so they gave me this here long coat with gold bars on the shoulders, and here I am."

"You're kind to offer your services to …" he paused and glanced at Carrie, "the lady here."

"Thank you, sir," replied the lieutenant with a hint of pride.

When they were out of the lieutenant's earshot, the general looked at Carrie. "It occurs to me that if I am going to vouch for you and help you obtain a pass, it would be useful to know your name."

"Oh! It's Carrie, Carrie Blaylock."

"Would that be 'miss' or 'misses?'"

"Miss."

***

Before the war dismantled Middle Tennessee's social order, the region's elite sent their daughters to the Nashville Female Academy. It stood off Church Street just east of the depot, and the sight of it shocked Carrie. She'd heard the Federal army had taken it over for a hospital, but still, she hadn't expected it to be in such a state. Her mind went to Collins D. Elliott, the school's headmaster, and how horrified he must be. It would be difficult to find anyone more devoted to the Southern cause.

Tents and crude shelters rose from the formal garden where Carrie had spent so many pleasant Sunday afternoons. Or had she? She'd sensed lately that the war was peeling away the smothering veneer of convention, and thinking back on it, she wasn't so sure that she really had enjoyed those Sundays when the boys came calling. Frivolous conversation didn't come naturally to her. She would have been perfectly content to remain in her room reading or drawing. And the clothes they had to wear. Even back then she'd branded hoop skirts as about the silliest fashion trend since powdered wigs.

Walking east from her old school, the sights and smells on Church Street heightened Carrie's discomfort. If she hadn't seen it, she wouldn't have believed it: soldiers and civilians alike were relieving themselves right in the street. The disgusting odor from that and from the droppings of countless horses, mules, and oxen made her aware of the urgent feeling in her stomach.

Groups of Negroes—men, women, and children—pressed around open fires on a vacant lot next to crude shanties of scrap lumber and discarded army tents. Seeing children with no shoes on this cold winter day, Carrie was hit by a wave of sadness. Her father was no abolitionist, but he held firm to the belief that treating fellow humans as chattel was contrary to God's will, a view Carrie accepted without question, though she didn't like to discuss it. But still, wouldn't these pitiful refugees be better off back on the farms where at least they might have food, shelter, and clothing?

When they came to High Street, Carrie shifted her vision to the State Capitol standing like a giant Greek temple atop Cedar Knob. A girl at the academy said once that Carrie admired the building because it was how she viewed herself: orderly, balanced, and symmetrical. That was then, Carrie thought; not much order, balance, and symmetry in my life these days. She'd heard the Yankee army was calling it "Fort Johnson" after the fiercely Unionist East Tennessean, Andrew Johnson, who now occupied the building as President Lincoln's military governor. Cannon and tents surrounded it.

Suddenly a weird sensation came over her. The landmarks were all familiar, but Nashville was a different place. For a scary instant, she didn't remember where she was and heard her mother trying to talk her out of the trip as clearly as if Amanda Blaylock was standing next to her.

Then her heart pumped even faster. Walking toward her down High Street was an old school friend, Ida Mabry, along with Ida's sister and her sister's two children. What if Ida recognizes me, Carrie thought. A girl in Murfreesboro had been shunned during the first Federal occupation for befriending Yankees, and here she was walking down Nashville's main street with a general carrying her bag. Carrie lowered her head to continue up Church Street, praying that the big sunbonnet was an adequate disguise, but fearful that any second she'd hear Ida call her name. A little further on, Carrie turned back for a look. Ida had apparently turned west on Church Street. Carrie didn't see her.

***

The tautness in Carrie's neck loosened slightly when she and the general finally arrived at the Forbeses' house on Cherry Street. The Forbeses occupied the left half of a two-sided brick town house close by the sidewalk. Its three stories included a top floor with dormers where Carrie had stayed during her school years. She announced her arrival with the brass knocker.

The heavy oak door swung open, and there stood Isabella Forbes. "Carrie, you're here. Lord, child, what have you done to yourself?"

Carrie had forgotten about the scratch. "I'll explain later."

Taking off her out-of-place sunbonnet, Carrie turned to the uniformed man on the sidewalk. He climbed the steps with her bag.

"This is General Charles Bradley. He was kind enough to escort me from the depot and help me get my pass."

The general removed his wide-brimmed campaign hat.

"Won't you come in, General?" Mrs. Forbes asked.

"Thank you, ma'am, but I've another train to catch."

"He's on his way up to Ohio on furlough to visit his family," Carrie said.

"Not even for a little refreshment to help you on your way?"

"Thank you, but I really must be going."

"Very well, General, you have a safe trip." Mrs. Forbes returned inside with Carrie's bag, leaving her at the door.

"Goodbye, Miss Blaylock. I hope the visit meets your expectations." The general replaced his hat and returned to his bag on the sidewalk. He hadn't taken more than a few steps when Carrie called after him.

"General."

He stopped to look back. She pulled the door shut, gathered her skirt, and trotted down the steps. "Thank you for being so kind. If I seemed distant at times, allow me to apologize."

"You haven't seemed distant. You've brightened my day considerably. It is I who should thank you." He removed his hat and looked into her eyes. "We won't start another campaign until spring, so perhaps our paths will cross when I return." He replaced his hat and turned to continue along Cherry Street.

Carrie followed him with her eyes until he was out of sight.

***

"Oh Carrie, I've talked half the night and ignored your life completely," said Lizzy Forbes. The Forbeses had let out Carrie's old, third-floor room to some army contract surgeons, so she was sharing Lizzy's bed in her second-floor room. Carrie wasn't surprised Lizzy had gone on so. Mrs. Forbes said once that if she added up all the talk from the two of them and divided it by two, she'd have girls who each talked about the right amount.

"What's it been like?" Lizzy asked.

Carrie hadn't made this trip to relive the horror, sorrow, and deprivation of the past two years. So she only skimmed the surface. She shared with Lizzy the division of labor around their house and farm, but didn't bring up the chronic shortages of food, cloth, and most everything else needed to survive. When it came to the battle, she only mentioned how incredibly loud it was.

"I know," Lizzy said. "We heard it here, thirty miles away."

The nearest Carrie came to complaining was sharing the unpredictability of their lives. "I'm suspended in perpetual uncertainty," Carrie said, "which feels worse than the grief, if you can believe that." She feared Lizzy would conclude that the war had hardened her into heartlessness the way she was so cursory in describing the loss of her father, her brother Travis, and Grantland, the man she'd planned to marry.

The mention of Grantland prompted a question from Lizzy. "Do you wonder now who you'll marry?"

Carrie lay quietly and reflected. "I've thought about it, sure."

"Has there been anyone else?"

"No. Well, yes, sort of, briefly. An artillery battery from Louisiana camped in our orchard during the six weeks our army was back, and I … I became acquainted with one of them, a first lieutenant."

"Only acquainted?"

"I went with him to a Christmas party." Carrie felt her heart race for an instant and was glad for the darkness hiding her blushing.

"What happened to him in the battle?"

"I have no idea."

"Let's hope he survived."

"Yes, let's hope." Carrie paused to collect her thoughts. "My attitude about marriage is changing, Lizzy. I resisted it at first. You remember Dr. Elliott's pledge: 'We educate every girl according to God's Word and demand of every fiber of her mind to be a wife, to be a mother.' Goodness, how many times did we hear that? But I don't see that as my path anymore."

Lizzy rolled onto her side, rested her head on her elbow, and asked Carrie what she meant.

"Marriage and motherhood aren't everything. The war seems to have laid bare thoughts and ideas hidden behind the curtain of convention and expectations. I've come around to thinking that I've always wanted more out of life than being subordinate to a man. I'm no longer willing to define myself that way. I'm getting comfortable with the prospect of being independent, maybe even living on my own."

"But who would support you?"

"I hope I could support myself."

"But how?"

"You know better than I that women are doing work now that they wouldn't have dreamed of before the war."

When Lizzy remarked that she wouldn't want to tend to wounded soldiers for the rest of her life, or be a government clerk or a factory girl, Carrie said she'd thought about teaching. "Women up North are teaching, and they will in the

South, too, regardless of how the war turns out. It'll be the women who educate children. And I think I'd be good at it."

"Those teachers up North don't lead very full lives, from what I hear. The pay is low, and they're often confined to tiny quarters, not much better than indentured servants," Lizzy said.

"It might be a struggle, but I'm willing to give it a try. And who knows, maybe someday I'll have my own school."

"So you'll never marry?"

"I didn't say that. It's just that I want more out of life. Perhaps I'll find a man who'll be content to let me have my own life."

She'd had some of the same thoughts, Lizzy said, but emphasized that she wanted a husband more than anything.

"Well you'll come closer to finding one here than any of us will in Murfreesboro now, unless we're willing to settle for a widower twice our age or a boy half our age, or a …"

"Or a what?"

"A Yankee," Carrie said with a little laugh.

Lizzy rolled onto her back and pulled her side of the covers up to her neck. There was no talk for a few minutes. "I've taken some comfort there."

"Where?"

"Yankees."

"Your family's Unionist. That seems natural."

"Some of our friends don't think so. Maryanne won't even speak to me anymore. "

"How can you avoid talking to Yankees? They're everywhere around here."

"It's more than talking," said Lizzy in a low voice.

"Lizzy, do you have a beau?"

Lizzy didn't reply.

Carrie lifted herself onto her elbows and looked in Lizzy's direction. "You do, don't you? Why haven't you told me?"

"I was afraid you'd think ill of me. I mean, your brother and Grantland and all. You'll meet him tomorrow. He walks me home from church and usually stays for dinner."

"And?"

"We don't get to spend much time together, mostly reading aloud on Sunday afternoons."

"Is he a soldier?"

"Sort of. He's the assistant surgeon, in charge of several hospitals."

"And?"

"His name is Gunter Schultz. A widower, but not one of those old men. He's thirty-two and has a little boy staying with the grandmother back home."

"Where's home?"

"Cincinnati. He's German. He came to America as a boy."

There was a long pause before Lizzy went on. "I worry that his circumstance clouds his judgment. If we married, the boy would likely come to live with us."

Ah, the lonely soldier Mother warned me about, Carrie thought. "You wouldn't be the first woman to marry a widower looking for someone to care for children. We know girls like that who have happy marriages."

"And we know some who don't."

"Has he proposed?"

"Yes. I told him I couldn't give him an answer until after the war. But I'm having second thoughts."

"About marrying him?"

"About putting off my acceptance. The war's already gone on much longer than anyone expected."

Carrie lay on her back again and pulled up the covers. Marrying a widower with a child had never crossed her mind.

They lay in silence until sleep overtook them.

***

"The pickings are slim, but I always manage to find something," Isabella Forbes said. With her market tote under her arm, she opened the front door to a gust of February air. "You enjoy your peace and quiet."

Carrie leaned against the closed door rubbing the back of her neck. I can use some peace and quiet, she thought.

Reading was the one diversion she counted on to relieve the tormenting uncertainty that was now her constant companion, so in the Forbeses' library she turned her attention to the shelves of books. She was methodical. Am I not always, she thought. She studied the titles from the upper left to the bottom right, compiling in her mind a list of a few books she'd ask to borrow.

The winter sun climbing above the buildings across Cherry Street flooded the room, so Carrie turned the stuffed chair to the window, eased into it, and waited to feel the soothing effects of the rays on her face. But she wasn't soothed. Her mind churned with images of the attack on the train and accepting the kindness of the young general. It felt disloyal. Disloyal to what? She wasn't sure. Disloyal to the cause? But do I even believe in the cause anymore? Did I ever? I just want it to end. More than anything, I just want it over.

With her eyes focused on her folded hands in her lap, Carrie's mind darted back to Christmas night, to the wine that had loosened propriety's grip on her. She was the girl mothers wanted their daughters to be like, yet she hadn't felt even the slightest twinge of guilt about it, which surprised her. Sitting alone in the quiet of the Forbeses' home brought back some of the glow of that night.

Less than a week later, on the morning of December 31, 1862, the two big Western armies slammed into each other within a few miles of the Blaylocks' farm. Carrie endured it with a calmness and efficiency she couldn't have predicted, though alone with her thoughts in the Forbeses' empty house, she was starting to feel it, feel what it was like to be surrounded by such terror and suffering.

At the end of the first day's fighting, some wounded Confederates managed to get across the Stones River to the Blaylocks' house, about seven of them. She and the others cared for the boys as best they could. Carrie hardly slept for three days and nights. On the third day Carrie's mother sent Sampson, the black boy, to town to fetch a surgeon. He returned with an orderly. The poor old fellow had only one good eye, and for a coat, he wore a blanket wrapped around him. The surgeons were too busy, he said, but he'd take the boys to town if he had a way. So Amanda Blaylock loaned him their carriage. That was the last they saw of the carriage and the two horses.

After the Federal army marched into Murfreesboro on January 5, General Rosecrans decreed that the wounded the Rebels left behind would all be collected at the female seminary under the care of a captured Confederate surgeon. Nearly every day throughout January, Carrie joined the other women and girls in Murfreesboro ministering to them. Eventually, the ones who could get around were paroled, while the others were brought to Nashville.

Now in the safety of the Forbeses' library, the horror of it all bubbled up and overflowed. Carrie burst out crying, all at once, with no anticipatory tears stinging her eyes. She shook violently from the crown of her head to the tip of her toes trying to control herself, but she couldn't. She sobbed until there was nothing left.

Wiping her eyes on the sleeve of her dress, she turned back to the books, found the right one, and lost herself in it.

***

Yesterday, on Sunday, Lizzy and Gunter had returned from the Washington's Birthday Parade in time for the dinner that Carrie had helped Mrs. Forbes prepare. Carrie baked some cornbread—there was no wheat flour in the house—which Mrs. Forbes served with ham, sweet potatoes, and buttermilk.

"The meal's sorely lacking in green vegetables," Mrs. Forbes said, "but it's filling, and that's more than can be said for a lot of meals served in Middle Tennessee these days."

With a trace of Ulster-Scot accent, she added, "and we're grateful to God for it, so we are."

Gunter Schultz seemed comfortable around the Forbeses, and Carrie surmised it was because he was a doctor like Lizzy's father. The army surgeon was attentive and courteous to her friend, which calmed Carrie's concern about the "lonely soldier." In fact, she thought, he doesn't seem like a soldier at all.

Dr. and Mrs. Forbes left after dinner to call on a Mrs. Pearl, the wife of Nashville's pre-war school superintendent. He was a pro-Union man who'd left town with his daughters to escape harassment from the pro-Confederate majority that was so vocal before Federal troops marched in following the loss of Fort Donelson. But a son had cast his lot with the South and was in the army, and Mrs. Pearl stayed behind.

So sad, Carrie thought. Her father's warnings against secession echoed again in her mind.

After Sunday dinner, Lizzy, Gunter, and Carrie had settled into the parlor where Lizzy offered to start a new book, but Carrie was content to join where they'd left off. Lizzy was like Carrie; she loved books and loved reading. Gunter's willingness to favor Lizzy with his presence while she lost herself in reading assured Carrie even more about their relationship.

***

Nearly two years of wartime deprivation had forced Carrie Blaylock to make up for the domestic deficiencies that came from growing up in a well-off household where servants did the cooking. So on Monday when Mrs. Forbes brought home two live hens in a makeshift cage of honeysuckle vines, Carrie knew what to do. She changed into her traveling dress, covered herself with an apron, and took the chickens out back. She snatched one up by the neck and swung it around like a windmill until she heard the click of its head snapping in her hand. Using her blood-soaked hand, she did the same with the other. Both birds ran around pumping blood from their headless necks, and when the second one gave out, she piled their warm bodies on the tangle of vines and took them inside.

She dropped them into the pot Mrs. Forbes had put on to boil, and when they were fully soaked, Carrie plucked the feathers, gutted them, and chopped apart their carcasses. The stew Lizzy's mother was making with these pitiful fowls and some carrots and potatoes she'd found would feed them for several days.

Around the dinner table that night, they discussed the dwindling number of women who still refused to go out on Nashville's crowded sidewalks without a male escort. It was usually safe during the daylight, the Forbeses all agreed. Lizzy, after all, walked alone to and from her work as a hospital matron, and her mother went out to market by herself. Dr. Forbes cautioned Carrie to stay away from the saloons down by Broad Street. Some of the soldiers and the multitude of civilian workers who'd flooded into Nashville had mistaken ladies for public women and propositioned them.

Carrie recalled during the discussion how the walk from the depot had unnerved her, even with the general as her escort. But I've made my choice, she told herself. I made it when I decided to take this trip alone. And I'm not turning back.

***

Captain John Lockridge stretched out on his folding cot under the canvas roof of the slab-sided hovel that passed for his winter quarters just outside Murfreesboro. The light of the coal oil lamp wasn't bright, but it offered enough illumination for him to do what he did every night now that he had a dry place to lay his head; he read the latest letter from the woman he'd recently committed to marry. This was the captain's ninth day reading Miranda Escobar's letter of February 10, 1863.

There was more to endlessly reading the letters than trying to stay in touch with her in his mind. It kept him from stewing so much about the increasingly rancorous dispute over President Lincoln's proclamation emancipating slaves. The captain fully supported it. But many didn't, and there was concern that something of a civil war might break out in the big Western army. One officer in particular, a major in a Southern Indiana regiment, had it in for Captain Lockridge and vowed to make his life miserable if he continued to speak out in favor of the president. "Watch your backside, Lockridge," a friendly captain in the Indiana regiment had warned. "The major really has it in for you."

The captain's tent mate, First Lieutenant Samuel L. Marshall made it his practice to keep a daily journal, and when he'd written all he cared to for Tuesday, February 24, 1863, he folded his leather-bound notebook and looked over to the captain.

"So, Lockridge, where'd you go today?"

"On a mission," the captain responded flatly while holding his fiancée's letter.

"Mission? What kind of mission?"

"Nothing you need to know about."

"My, aren't you testy?"

The captain didn't say anything at first but then turned to his friend. "If I tell you, you must not breathe a word of it to anyone."

"Fair enough," the lieutenant said. "So tell me about the mission."

"I went to see a widow woman about some stolen pigs."

"You what?"

"You heard me."

"Why in the world would you do something like that?"

"Orders."

"Orders from who?"

"Who do you think?"

"Bradley? He's not even here."

"He sent a dispatch by the wire."

"Why?"

"It seems he believes the family's loyal."

"I'll bet. Like most of the supposed loyalists around here, miraculously changed color from gray to blue when the Rebs evacuated. But how did Bradley find out about something so trivial?"

"I have no idea, but I went."

"That is embarrassing. Did the widow dip snuff?"

The captain hesitated. "She wasn't what I expected." His first impression of the Widow Blaylock was how stunningly handsome she was, possessed of a dark, almost Creole appearance that was accented by her silver hair. She was as dignified as any woman he'd ever met, and even in the deprivation of the current circumstance, her countenance was one of elegance. He estimated her age to be around his mother's, early fifties. When Marshall asked Lockridge if her husband had died in the war, the captain said he didn't think so, given her age. But he speculated that her son had. The widow told him her son would be his age if he were still living, but she didn't say how he'd died.

"It would be rare for a Union boy to come out of this secesh-infested place," First Lieutenant Marshall said.

"Maybe her son was in the Rebel army; there are plenty of divided families in Tennessee."

"Bradley would never send any of us to help a widow if he knew she had a Johnnie for a son."

"Yeah, it doesn't add up. And besides, as best I can determine, a loyal family wouldn't have lasted around here. Maybe I'll find out more."

"You're going back?"

"The widow didn't see anything; it was her daughter."

"So the widow has a daughter?"

"Two, actually, the one I met today and an older one who's away. She's the one I need to talk to."

"Is she pretty?"

"I just said she's away."

"I mean the one you met today."

"You know, she really is."

"Maybe you'll need some help on your next visit."

"She's just a girl, Marshall, fourteen or fifteen. You'll have to come back in a few years."

"Lockridge, let me tell you something; if I make it out of this war in one piece, I'll never so much as set foot on the south bank of the Ohio River; I don't care how many pretty Southern girls want me."

The captain returned to his fiancée's letter, but his attention wasn't on it. It was on his visit to the Widow Blaylock's. The day definitely was ending better than it had started.

***

"Pigs, sir?"

"That's right Captain, pigs."

"I'm to investigate a theft of pigs from some widow woman?"

"This is all I know; it came in by the wire late yesterday."

The brigade chief of staff handed a dispatch to the captain.

Louisville, Ky.
February 22, 1863

Maj. Henderson,
Chief of Staff etc.

Send a member of my staff to investigate the theft of pigs from a Widow Blaylock, who I believe to be a loyal citizen. She lives on a farm outside M'boro.

Charles Bradley
Brigadier General
Cmdng Brigade

***

The first person the captain had asked when he reached the Courthouse Square directed him to the Blaylock farm: about a mile out the Salem Pike backing up to the Stones River. That was welcome news. There were rumors that bushwhackers managed to penetrate the Union lines now and then, and the river would give him protection on this solo excursion.

Arriving at the river, Captain Lockridge knew he'd missed the farm. Riding back, he saw why. The turnoff was barely visible, a narrow passage penetrating one of the cedar thickets that seemed to be everywhere around Murfreesboro. The lane slanted diagonally off the pike, emerged from the evergreens, and then cut to the right through an orchard. The crusts of ice on the potholes told him he was the first person to travel the lane that morning. He spotted the house cresting a slight rise beyond the barren fruit trees.

He sometimes felt sorry for folks living round here, even if they were mostly pro-Confederacy. Before the Rebels retreated after the battle, it had been a year of continuous back and forth. The Rebel army moved into the area early in 1862 after its defeat at Fort Donelson and the fall of Nashville. When they retreated farther south, the pursuing Federals occupied Murfreesboro. That summer, Forrest's Confederate cavalry took over the town. When those Rebels left, the Federals returned, only to abandon Murfreesboro in late summer to check the Confederate invasion of Kentucky. After that deadly debacle, General Braxton Bragg located his Southern army at Murfreesboro and stayed through November and December. Now the winter camps and fortifications of the entire Union Army of the Cumberland spread out around the town that had once been Tennessee's capital, overwhelming the local population.

It's enough to make my head swim, the captain said to himself, like that town in Virginia, Winchester.

Captain Lockridge concluded from the look of the place that these folks had it better than most. That's odd, he thought. If they're loyal as reported, then surely their neighbors would have run them off. Most of Middle Tennessee's loyalists had taken refuge in Union-occupied Nashville, and their houses had either been burned or taken over by the less fortunate or by the Negroes who were emboldened to seek freedom now that the Federal army was around.

It was a sturdy, two-story, white-framed house with a one-story portico, similar to so many houses he'd seen in Tennessee and Kentucky. The porch held four rocking chairs that gave off an air of loneliness on this cold day. There were two windows on either side of the porch and five windows across the second story. Bulky limestone chimneys flanked the house, one emitting bluish wood smoke that quickly got lost in the low, gray sky.

Off to the left stood a log barn with a nearby smokehouse and a pen enclosed by sticks held together with vines. A pigless pigpen, he thought, chuckling. Past the barn was a cabin he assumed was a slave dwelling. He still couldn't get used to what he'd discovered when he first crossed the Ohio River into Kentucky: pro-Union slave-owners. The fences were missing—as they were from every farm, long ago pilfered for firewood—but otherwise the place had a tidy look he wouldn't expect on a farm without men left to do the heavy work. But then, he thought, I don't know for sure that there are no men around.

The sky started spitting bits of snow or ice, he couldn't tell which, as he pulled up to a hitching post on the barn side of the house. Turning around after securing his horse, he saw for the first time a boy standing next to the barn door by a pile of split wood. He clutched an ax in one hand. A startled Negro woman emerged from the barn and stood alongside him.

The captain tipped his hat, walked to the front of the house, and climbed the steps to the door. The boy and the woman followed. Reaching the door, he looked back and saw the boy holding the ax across his chest like a soldier carrying a weapon into battle. He was a strong-looking black boy of maybe sixteen or seventeen.

Wouldn't that be something, thought the captain, come down here and get myself axed to death by the very people I hope to liberate. The hot-headed, anti-abolition major would get a big laugh out of it, as would so many others who didn't have any use for those who supported the president's proclamation. And plenty of the men didn't have much use for staff officers of any political persuasion.

Captain Lockridge stood sideways to the door, keeping an eye on the boy and the woman. He knocked and then lowered his hand to the holster carrying his Colt Navy revolver.

The door cracked, and a girl looked up at him.

"What do you want?"

"I've been sent by General Bradley to investigate the theft of some pigs. Is the Widow Blaylock in?"

"Wait here." She shut the door. Then it opened again revealing the form of a grown woman.

"Are you the Widow Blaylock?"

"I am."

"I've been sent by General Bradley to look into a theft of pigs."

The door opened wider, and Amanda Blaylock looked past him toward the boy and woman. "That's all right, Sampson." The captain turned to see the boy lowering the ax.

"Please come in."

Closing the door behind him, he removed his hat, a gesture not all his fellow soldiers would make. He felt satisfied with himself, recalling his mother's admonition when he went off to war: "Now, you behave like a gentleman down there."

"Please come into the parlor, Captain," the woman said, opening a door to the right off the central hallway. The instant she closed the door, it opened again, and the girl walked in and closed the door behind her.

"Have a seat." The Widow Blaylock pointed to the stuffed chair. Well-placed to catch the light from the window, he thought. For reading. She and the girl sat on the long settee against the opposite wall. They'd been knitting, he surmised from the colorless yarn and needles resting between them.

"Amanda Blaylock, Captain, and this is my daughter Sarah," the lady said confidently.

"Hello, Sarah." The girl didn't speak, but kept her eyes trained on him with an expression that he couldn't read.

"I'm Captain John Lockridge from General Bradley's staff and … ah, I've been sent to investigate … ah … the supposed theft of your pigs by soldiers."

The fire in the big fireplace and the vivid yellow-flowered wallpaper gave the room a warm glow even on this cold gray day. An unexpected feeling flowed through him. Home.

"The life of a volunteer officer isn't completely unknown to me. I imagine you don't consider this a plumb assignment, investigating a theft of pigs," said Mrs. Blaylock, smiling slightly.

He couldn't help from smiling back at her, not quite sure what to say. "Truthfully Mrs. Blaylock, I don't."

"We'll try to make the most of your visit. Can I offer you some tea? Or what passes for tea around here these days?"

"That would be nice."

"Sarah, pour us some tea."

The girl left the room and returned right away with two sets of cups and saucers that reminded the captain of the fine china his mother brought out on special occasions. The girl took a potholder from the table at the end of the settee, gripped the pot hanging over the fire, and poured the steaming liquid. She handed her mother a cup and then one to the captain. She looked him in the eye for an instant after he took the cup. The skirt of her dress brushed against his boots. Is the girl really that pretty, he thought, or have I just been away from feminine company too long?

The widow took a sip of her tea. "What do you want to know?"

"Tell me what you saw," he said.

"I wasn't at home. It was my daughter who encountered the thieves."

"Well then, Sarah, tell me about it."

"It wasn't me, sir; it was my older sister." The girl kept her brown eyes on him with the same expression on her face.

"Then I'd better talk to her."

"She's away in Nashville, visiting friends," Amanda Blaylock said.

"When do you expect them to return?" He felt awkward, like a little boy.

"Them?"

"I assume she's traveling with her husband."

He noticed a frown come over the widow's face.

"She has no husband. She's developed quite an independent streak, and she's traveling alone. As for when she'll return, your guess is as good as mine, given the uncertainty of travel these days."

"I take it that she's older than Sarah?"

"Closer to your age, which I judge to be mid-twenties."

"Twenty-five." The captain liked the drift of the conversation, away from pigs.

"My son would be the same age had he survived."

Captain Lockridge felt awkward again and turned to study the room. The bookcases covering the wall on either side of the door were full of leather-bound books with their titles displayed on their spines in gold print. It reminded him how deprived he was of something decent to read. He turned his gaze back to the widow. "Would one time be better than another to catch your daughter when she returns from Nashville?"

"Sundays." He detected a trace of sadness in her voice.

There didn't seem to be much more to say, but the captain didn't want to leave. It had been a while since he'd felt this level of contentment—since he was home on furlough, in fact. He struggled for something to say that might lead to further conversation. He didn't have to.

"Tell me about yourself," Mrs. Blaylock said in a motherly tone.

He came from Columbus, Ohio, he told her, the second of three children. When she asked about his occupation in civilian life and he told her he was a lawyer, she stared at him silently for what seemed like a minute.

"My son was a lawyer."

"Here in Murfreesboro?"

"Yes."

He suspected from her accent that she was not originally from these parts. From Philadelphia, she said in response to his inquiry. Her husband was a minister in the Episcopal Church, and they moved to Murfreesboro in the early 1850s to start the new church.

"My father is a minister in the Episcopal Church."

"What a coincidence. In Columbus?"

"Yes."

There was a pause, and the Widow Blaylock looked at him silently. Her eyes seemed to be filling with tears. "Tell me about the rest of your family," she said.

His parents were both living. He had two sisters, one older, one younger, both married, and both their husbands were in Grant's army in Mississippi.

"The war has certainly touched your family. No wife?"

"I'm engaged to be married."

The captain wanted to know what caused her son's death, but decided it was best to leave that alone. It could be anything in these dreadful times. And her husband, what happened to him? He saw tears glistening in the widow's eyes again and decided it was time to leave. "I must be going."

"'Very well." She stood, opened the parlor door, and the three of them walked to the front of the house. The girl hadn't taken her eyes off him for a second.

"By the way, Captain, I'm sorry if Sampson startled you. He's as protective of me as he is of his own mother, and this is his homeplace too, you know."

A thought entered the captain's mind. "I'm wondering, Mrs. Blaylock, how did the pig thieves get past the boy without hurting him?"

"He wasn't here. It was on a Sunday afternoon, and we're seldom here on Sunday afternoon. We all go to town."

"But I thought you said Sunday was a good time to catch your older daughter."

"She doesn't go to town with us anymore on Sundays."

***

Surgeon Gunter Schultz came to the Forbeses' Nashville home for dinner again on Tuesday and brought a friend. Carrie thought nothing of it at first, but later, when they retired to the parlor, she figured it out. Lizzy had set it up for her to meet the man. Carrie suppressed her anger, and as the four of them passed a pleasant evening, more charitable thoughts emerged. Lizzy was only trying to be kind.

His name was Dexter Hobson, a merchant in his family's dry goods business who was now the army's assistant quartermaster in Nashville. It was an important job, for Major General Rosecrans was transforming Tennessee's capital city into the principal Western supply depot for the Union army. Like Gunter Schultz, Hobson wore the uniform of a major, but he'd never fired a weapon, at least not in the army.

His appearance intrigued Carrie. His shiny black hair was parted down the middle, and he wore a thin mustache and an equally thin goatee under his lower lip. He reminded her of a character in a book, but she couldn't recall which one. The man was so outspoken in his political views that Carrie feared he might offend the Forbeses.

"I've got no use for abolitionists and little use for Abe Lincoln," he stated at dinner. "If he goes any further making this war about slavery, I shall resign my commission and return to St. Louis where there's a small fortune to be made in government contracts. And I'll tell you *another* man I've no use for and that's Andrew Johnson. His constant meddling in military affairs isn't helping. He gives Old Rosey fits sometimes, but the general's smart. He just ignores him."

The major turned to Carrie. "What about you, Miss Blaylock? Where does your family come down on Andrew Johnson?"

Carrie had to think fast. "He's not well-regarded in my circles."

Lizzy turned away to try to keep from laughing.

The man was engaging, and his sense of humor allowed them all to look past his strong political pronouncements. It had been a long time since Carrie had such a good laugh. Still, she was eager for the evening to end. More talk would only increase the chance she'd let something slip. Carrie suspected that Gunter knew about Travis and about Grantland, and she warmed to him even more, observing how careful he was not to say anything in front of this major that might cause her any distress.

As Gunter and Major Hobson stood at the front door ready to leave, Major Hobson looked down at Carrie. He was a tall man, standing over six feet.

"There's a concert tomorrow night at the Adelphi, Miss Blaylock, and I'd be honored for you to accompany me."

Carrie's heart pounded. She felt her face go red, and she could hardly speak. But she did. "I'd be delighted."

"Good, I shall be by at 6:30," said Major Dexter Hobson with a broad grin that made his goatee stick out.

***

Carrie leaned against the door as it shut, struggling to catch her breath.

"Are you all right?" Lizzy sounded concerned.

"No I'm not all right. Look what I've done, accepted an invitation to go out on the town with a Yankee soldier. I spent four years of my life here. If someone sees me and it gets back to Murfreesboro, my life will be worse than it already is."

They stood by the door while Carrie caught her breath, and then returned to the parlor. Carrie sat on the edge of the sofa with her legs drawn up, clasping her hands in her lap. "What am I going to do?"

Lizzy hesitated before answering. "You responded favorably to his invitation."

"Was I mad? What got into me?"

Lizzy paused again. "Something made you say 'yes.'"

Carrie leaned back, stretched her legs in front of her, and stared at the smoldering fire. Her voice was barely audible. "I suppose you're right."

"Perhaps you miss a man in your life more than you're willing to admit to yourself. Perhaps you're lonely."

Carrie's eyes stayed fixed on the fire. "You believe that, don't you?"

"What?"

"That I'm lonely."

"It's crossed my mind."

"And you arranged to have that man here because you thought it would make me feel better."

"I asked Gunter to invite someone, a man who has no wife."

"We don't know that he has no wife."

"Gunter would not invite a married man, at least not knowingly."

Carrie kept her gaze on the hot coals. "We really don't know much about him."

"You're only going to an evening concert."

"What would you guess his age, thirty?"

"Something like that, about Gunter's age."

"He seemed gentlemanly enough."

"He is a gentleman, Carrie, and he liked you."

"But he doesn't know a thing about me. He thinks I'm loyal, like you."

Lizzy laughed.

"What's funny?"

"The way you responded to his question about Andrew Johnson: 'Not popular in my circles.' That's one of your best lines ever."

Carrie looked up and spoke louder. "I thought so, too, if I do say so myself."

"Can't you be equally cunning tomorrow night? You don't have to tell him much of anything about yourself."

"I suppose you're right."

"Maybe you'll enjoy his company and have a pleasant evening."

Carrie closed her eyes. "Perhaps I will."

***

Wartime rumors swept through Nashville as regularly as waves on the ocean, and the latest was that bolts of cloth had come in on a train from Louisville and would be hauled to Zibart's Dry Goods Store on Market Street. The doors would be thrown open at noon. Months had passed since there'd been any cloth or much of anything else for sale in Nashville. General Rosecrans reserved his vulnerable lifeline north for military use, but at Andrew Johnson's urging, the department commander eased up after his army went into winter quarters around Murfreesboro. Candles, cloth, buttons, thread, and hardware began to arrive, if only in a trickle.

When Carrie picked up the rumor about the cloth for sale, an idea popped into her head. The Blaylocks hadn't enjoyed the comfort of sleeping under sheets since the battle. They'd torn up theirs for bandages for the wounded. She decided she'd walk down to Market Street and see for herself if the rumor about the shipment was true. If it was, she'd buy cloth to take home for sheets.

***

The soothing warmth of the sun that Carrie had counted on Monday to calm her wasn't available Wednesday. A thick layer of clouds cast a gray pall over the city overflowing with the detritus of war. Carrie sat by herself in the Forbeses' library and fretted. It's so unlike me, she thought. I'm usually so cautious, too cautious my friends say. She figured that about all she could do was look forward to the next day when the concert would be behind her. And I can learn from this mistake, she told herself.

The sound of Mrs. Forbes unlocking the front door interrupted Carrie's rambling thoughts. Only it wasn't Mrs. Forbes.

"Dr. Forbes."

"Hello Carrie."

The doctor stood in the hall looking toward her, removing his hat and coat.

"Time must have gotten away from me," she said, not expecting him for another half-hour.

"No, I'm early." He was there during his work day to accompany her to the bank.

The doctor took a seat opposite Carrie in the library. He didn't speak for at least a minute, which might have bred tension had it been anyone else, but she was accustomed to his reticent demeanor.

"I've come a wee bit early to have a word with you, alone."

He sat for a few seconds looking down at his hands folded on his lap before he looked up at her. "Intimate conversation doesn't come easily to me, and I may be intruding into an area that's out of bounds. If I am, I hope you'll stop me."

"I cannot imagine any topic you'd discuss with me that would be inappropriate."

"Aye, I hope not."

"What is it?"

He paused a second before he answered. "Your health."

Carrie sat quietly and listened.

"Please don't misunderstand me, you're as lovely as ever, but I cannot help but notice; you've fallen off. I'm concerned that you're not getting enough to eat. People are showing up now from the countryside, refugees who are not well-nourished. There's even talk of famine in Middle Tennessee."

Carrie thought for a few seconds before responding. She'd vowed never to complain about their condition. It was hard on everyone, and she looked to her mother's strength as an example. In the face of unimaginable losses, her mother never complained, not once.

"It's been difficult, Dr. Forbes, I won't deny that, but honestly, I believe we're making out better than many, maybe better than most."

"But it's likely to get worse. General Rosecrans is not General Buell. I'm sure you know about his order authorizing foraging."

"Oh sure, and we all know that the part about strict supervision by officers isn't being followed. They'll steal anything they can get their hands on. In fact, last month some soldiers stole our pigs." Carrie paused. "It's taken us a while to realize it, but actually, living inside the Federal lines now seems to be working to our advantage."

"Aye, it's the wretched folks in the no-man's land who are being picked over every day. One day it's the Federals and another day it's the Rebels. Something has to happen soon or we'll have a real disaster on our hands."

"And don't forget, Dr. Forbes, we have Cassie and Sampson. Cassie has taught us how to be farmers, and Sampson is strong and willing. "

"But they could walk off anytime."

"I really don't think Cassie and Sampson will leave, certainly not Cassie."

"Your father was good to them, and I'm sure they realize that."

"Cassie certainly does. We still have our milk cow, we still have the plough horse, and we have our wagon."

"You might not have your draught horse much longer, for I hear the army is requisitioning every horse and mule it can find."

"I don't know how we'd get by without at least one horse. How could we plow?"

"Aye, my point exactly. Conditions could get worse, and I doubt that being behind the lines will protect your horse. I'm sure the army has taken over homes in your area."

"At first only the ones vacated by families that fled with Bragg's army, but now they've started moving into houses of anyone they suspect is strong secessionist. I suppose not being in town and having a house not visible from the road has helped us. It's crossed my mind that if some officers boarded with us, some gentlemen, we might be better off."

"The Confederates could return, you know, there could be another battle."

"I wouldn't want to live through anything like that again, that's for sure. But the Federals are building defenses all around Murfreesboro, and they're getting stronger every day."

"It does seem likely that the next fight will be to the south. I suppose that's some consolation to you." Dr. Forbes sat for another minute before he spoke again. "Your sprits, Carrie, how are they? You've suffered terrible losses, you've witnessed things that no human should ever see, certainly no young lady."

"Dealing with the wounded after the battle hasn't bothered me as much as I would have thought. Losing Father and Travis has been difficult."

"And Grantland."

"Yes, and Grantland."

The losses are only part of it, Carrie knew, but she didn't want to worry Dr. Forbes any more than he already was. There were times when the uncertainly of it all felt like being ground between millstones.

"Has your mother given any thought to leaving?"

"She's mentioned it, yes. Now that we're behind Federal lines, we could travel to Philadelphia to be with her family, but she won't leave. We wouldn't have a place to come home to."

"I want you to know that you and your family are always welcome here. Nashville's no paradise, but you might be safer here. Will you assure me that you'll tell your mother that?"

"That's kind of you, and yes, I will tell her."

"I hope I haven't been too familiar with you."

"Oh no. I so appreciate your concern. It means a lot to me."

"Good. Now, shall we be on our way to the bank?"

***

Random snowflakes flew around Carrie and Dr. Forbes as they made their way down Church Street. They hadn't gone far before she detected the aroma of baking bread. The Louisville train must have brought flour too, she thought.

Carrie was about to learn firsthand another benefit of living behind Federal lines besides protection from outlaws: access to her mother's money.

"Good morning, Dr. Forbes," said the banker as the two of them walked in off the street. He was a short, round, bald man whose accent revealed his Northern roots, obviously one of many who'd flooded into Nashville to fill the vacuum left when the Federal army shut down the businesses of anyone suspected of supporting the Southern cause, and that was most of them. "This must be Miss Blaylock."

"Aye, so it is, Stooks."

"How do you do, madam," said the banker bowing slightly. "The Forbeses must feel blessed to have a lady of your charm lodging with them."

Let's just get down to business, Carrie thought. "Thank you."

"Please have a seat," said the man.

It had taken some doing, but with the help of Amanda Blaylock's brother in Philadelphia and Dr. Forbes's connections in Nashville, she'd arranged for Carrie to obtain U.S. currency. "I might as well make the most of it," her mother had said, accepting that she couldn't convince her oldest daughter not to make the Nashville trip without a proper escort.

When the transaction was complete and Carrie and Dr. Forbes returned to the sidewalk, he kindly insisted that she allow him to accompany her to Zibart's. "Thieves prey on large crowds, don't you know."

Carrie thanked him, but said she felt comfortable going by herself. It was only a short walk, and she could hire someone to help her bring home her purchases, assuming the rumor was true and assuming she'd find cloth to buy. And besides, she thought, he has more important work than helping me buy fabric.

"Aye, suit yourself," he said.

He looked up and down the street to make sure they weren't being watched. Satisfied that it was safe, Dr. Forbes peeled off some greenbacks for Carrie and pocketed the rest for safekeeping. Carrie put the notes in the pocket of her dress, said goodbye to him, and started on the walk down to Market Street. At least, she thought, if I keep my mind on not being robbed, I won't be worrying about my foolish acceptance of Major Hobson's invitation.

***

As the concert hour drew near, it dawned on Carrie that the trepidation plaguing her stemmed as much from insecurity over how to behave in a man's company as it did from the prospect of being spotted in public with a Federal officer. She'd never been out with any man before the artillery lieutenant on Christmas night, and that hardly counted, her mind was so clouded from oversampling the wine. Being with Grantland hardly counted either; they'd known each other for so long. She'd come to realize over the past few months that, although she was headed to the altar with him, perhaps blindly so, he'd been nothing more to her than a good friend.

Her forebodings, it turned out, proved to be misplaced. It was a splendid evening. The concert hall was packed with military people and civilians alike, but she didn't observe anyone who might recognize her. She lost herself in the rousing music and felt perfectly at ease with Major Hobson. A warm spot for him revealed itself unexpectedly on their walk home. She slid her hand inside his arm as they made their way along the sidewalk. Like a grown woman, she thought, perfectly capable of making my own decisions.

***

The cloud of uneasiness hovering over Carrie about traveling alone on Nashville's crowded streets had blown away completely by Thursday. Now it felt more like an adventure. So she struck out in search of flour. It would make a nice contribution to Mrs. Forbes if she could bring home a sack. But at the first store she visited she learned that only a few bags were made available to civilians, and they'd gone out the door within the first hour. Returning to the Forbeses' house, she hung up her cape and bonnet—the nice one that matched her cape, not the sunbonnet—and headed for the kitchen to give Mrs. Forbes the bad news.

"Not to worry dear," Lizzy's mother said, pointing to two sacks of flour resting on the counter. "I have no idea how your assistant quartermaster friend got his hands on them, but we don't ask those kinds of questions these days, no we don't. We take what we can get, so we do. There's one for us and one for you to carry home with you." She stopped what she was doing and turned to face Carrie. "You must have made quite an impression on him."

"Lonely soldiers are drawn to most any woman, Mother says."

"You've always sold yourself too short, my dear, when it comes to the stronger sex."

Carrie wasn't quite sure how to take that, but assumed she meant it as a compliment. "Thank you."

***

The unexpected took a bitter turn on Saturday. Two strangers, a man and a woman, presented themselves at the Forbeses' inquiring about a visitor from Murfreesboro. When Mrs. Forbes summoned Carrie to the door, they said they needed to speak to her. Alone. Lizzy's mother didn't like the looks of the strangers and suggested that Carrie shouldn't be with them by herself.

"Thank you, but I'll be fine," Carrie said. She draped her cape over herself and stepped down to the sidewalk. They introduced themselves as army detectives. Carrie was doubtful at first but recalled hearing that the ruthless army chief detective, William Truesdail, had taken to hiring women to do some of his dirty work. The woman spoke first, asking Carrie her name, why she was in Nashville, and when she planned to return home.

Then the man took over. "You've no doubt heard about the widespread smuggling. We're catching women now, sneaking out of Nashville with items useful to the Rebel army."

"We're not insinuating that you're here to violate the law," the woman broke in. "We just want to give you fair warning in case you're tempted."

"I hope you're not insinuating I'd pilfer medicines from Dr. Forbes," said Carrie, feeling anger replace her fear.

"We certainly hope not," the woman said harshly.

"It's more than medicine we're worried about, miss," said the man. "Nothing must leave Nashville that could be of value to the enemy. That includes arms, powder, ammunition, even food and clothing." He leaned closer to Carrie. "Or cloth that can be made into clothing."

Carrie said nothing.

"Do we make ourselves clear?" the woman said.

"I understand," Carrie responded.

"We'll be on our way, miss," said the man.

"And we'll be watching," said the woman.

Carrie stood alone in the cold for a minute to collect her thoughts. Did someone follow her out of Zibart's? Had the banker tipped them off?

As she climbed the steps, a sickening sensation took hold of her. Major Hobson?

***

It wasn't him. Major Hobson had shown up at the Forbeses' the next Sunday with an empty carpet bag. "It's big enough to hold your sack of flour and the cloth you bought." The opportunity to sleep under sheets and bake bread and biscuits wasn't worth the risk of being arrested for smuggling, Carrie told him, though she was careful to express her appreciation. There was no telling how many rules he'd violated giving them the flour.

"I have a plan," he said.

The wives of some generals and colonels had been arriving in Nashville over several days from their homes scattered across Ohio, Indiana, and Illinois. He'd been placed in charge of securing them lodging and seeing that they were delivered on to the front. He'd arranged for a separate ladies' car to take them on to Murfreesboro.

"I'm to be on the car with those wives?"

"That's my plan. No one will be searching their luggage."

"But won't it be obvious I don't belong?"

"They don't know each other. You'll be just another face in the crowd. If anyone asks, you shouldn't have any difficultly coming up with a convincing tale about who you are."

***

It had been a fretful night, Carrie's mind racing with endless possibilities of what could go wrong. The sunbonnet would be so out of place it would give her away. But if she didn't hide her face, the detectives would surely recognize her. A night of back and forth hadn't resolved the dilemma, so she made what felt like an impulsive decision Tuesday morning preparing to leave for the depot. She would have to dress the part.

She donned the nice blue dress she'd worn to the concert and borrowed a hat from Lizzy. She considered a veil, but that wouldn't fit on a car full of women. Smuggling hard currency was forbidden, as well, so Carrie got a needle and thread from Lizzy and stitched her roll of U.S. dollars into one of her petticoats. There were no reports of any searches of the person of a woman, at least not so far, but she wondered if that was still the case. Truesdail had started employing women detectives for a reason.

When Carrie and Dr. Forbes reached the depot, they spotted the gaggle of women congregating by the last car of a waiting train. Carrie carefully looked around and felt a sense of relief when she didn't see either of the two detectives. She did see Major Hobson. He was standing in the middle of the chatting ladies, and when he and Carrie spotted each other, he acknowledged her with a slight bow of his head. She returned the favor with a small smile.

Her affectionate gesture toward the major vanished abruptly. Standing two cars away and staring straight at her was the young lieutenant who'd confronted her about her pass. The boy hadn't seen much of her face that day, and she doubted he could recognize her. But he kept staring at her and then took a few steps toward her. To her relief, he stopped and turned away. She assumed he had better sense than to wade into a nest of high-ranking officers' wives even if he did recognize her.

She would be the wife of a young brigadier general from Sandusky, Ohio, she'd decided if anyone asked. But miraculously, no one did. Carrie passed her time on the trip sitting next to an older woman from Indiana who talked without stopping. In other circumstances this might have annoyed Carrie. It was a relief that the babbling woman never even took the time to ask who she was sitting next to.

Carrie's biggest difficulty, it turned out, was getting her loaded bags home from the Murfreesboro depot. She used a silver coin to pay a Negro boy to help her.

Carrie rolled around in bed that night unable to sleep. Something that had happened when she and her helper had walked away from the depot nagged her. The officer in charge of the station guards followed her with menacing eyes until she was out of his sight. Smuggling the flour and fabric might come back to haunt her, and if anyone got wind of the greenbacks, there was no telling what might happen.

CHAPTER THREE

March 1863

A robin's endless chattering aroused Carrie at first light on her first morning back at home. She craned her neck for a look out the window to see what kind of day it would be, but the pre-dawn gray didn't offer a clue. Most likely clear, her instinct told her. It felt terribly cold, the way it gets when the heat-trapping clouds drift to the east during the night. She pulled the comforter to her chin and contemplated her day. It would be different—not earth-shaking different, but different enough to give her something to look forward to. She could bake biscuits. And she had something new to read.

She lay watching her breath disappear in the cold morning air, and a thought arose more disconcerting than the prospect of being arrested for smuggling. It was her conversation with Lizzy Forbes about being lonely. Denial can be a balm that eases pain, Carrie had learned, but denial's comfort eventually wears off. Reality will set in. Often others see our reality first.

I might as well face it, she thought. I am lonely much of the time.

She dressed and made her way down the stairs and out to the kitchen. Her shabby, patched-up, wool coat kept her warm while she knelt on the floor and opened the fire box in the bulky, claw-footed, iron stove. She took the little tin shovel hanging nearby and scraped away the ashes covering last night's smoldering coals. Cassie had taught her this trick, and it hadn't failed Carrie yet.

Next to the stove was the wooden box Sampson kept filled with cedar shavings. Carrie grabbed a handful, piled them on the glimmering coals and then arranged four sticks of seasoned oak so they'd ignite from the burning kindling. When she was satisfied it would burn, she stood and reached for the heavy wool scarf hanging on a nail by the door.

This was her usual head covering at home on cold mornings, the plaid scarf that had been her father's. She draped it over her head, tied it snugly under her chin, and let herself out the kitchen door. The frayed rope holding the well bucket was stiff with ice, and it stung her bare hands as she fought to separate it.

A full bucket of well water was too heavy to lug into the kitchen, so after she cranked the bucket up, she poured half the water back. Even half a bucket was a strain. She wrapped both of her chapped hands around the handle and waddled up the steps with the bucket between her legs. She took an empty pot, set it on the floor, tipped the bucket to get the right amount of water, and then set the pot on the warming stove.

Carrie lifted the milk pail from its peg and returned outside. She eased her head around the corner of the kitchen house and peeked toward the orchard and the lane. She didn't see anything that she should be worried about, so she crunched across the frozen ground to the barn. The cedar logs it was built from years earlier still gave off a sweet aroma, and they'd never been chinked, so the spaces between them admitted enough light to find her way. Milk Cow was in her appointed stall. The work horse was in another. The two back ones where they'd stabled the carriage horses were vacant.

Nothing in her privileged life had hinted that she'd ever be doing the milking—or any of the other chores for that matter. The cook had always milked. But now Carrie was the cook. In truth, she'd come to like milking. The feel of the soft warm teats in her raw hands comforted her, and watching the bucket fill with frothy milk was an island of constancy in a sea of uncertainty. She did some of her best thinking sitting on the rustic three-legged stool. On this day, her first morning back from Nashville, she contemplated how she'd respond should a Yankee officer question her about the flour and fabric she'd smuggled home. And the greenbacks.

***

The Salem Pike was crowded the first Wednesday in March as it was every day now. Regiments trudged to and from picket duty, couriers and cavalrymen on horseback plodded along, and beaten-down teams of mules and horses struggled to pull wagons and artillery through the mud. Carrie sloshed along the path where the fences once ran. Her heart ached for the bedraggled Confederate prisoners being herded through the mire on their way to uncertain futures in damp, cold, disease-ridden, rat-infested prison camps up North.

Arriving at the Courthouse Square, she paused to discreetly raise her head for a look around. The Square was crammed with teamsters, horses, mules, wagons, cannon, and makeshift cabins rising randomly from the hog wallow that once was a lush green lawn. The sickening stench churned her innards. Peering from beneath her sunbonnet, she spotted a lone officer on the sidewalk diagonally across from her. When their eyes met, she thought she detected in him an intention to walk toward her, and the prospect of being arrested for smuggling brought a chill to the back of her neck.

She hurriedly debated her options. If I scurry away, it'll arouse his suspicion. But the longer I linger here, the more likely he is to walk over and question me. A third option popped into her head: go to him and engage him in some banal conversation. Surely he wouldn't expect a contraband smuggler, and a woman at that, to be so bold as to approach a Federal officer. As she drew nearer to the man, she picked out on his shoulder the silver bar of a first lieutenant. Carrie was about to say something to him when he turned away, stepped off the sidewalk, waded through the muck, and disappeared into the collection of shanties.

Trying to look as inconspicuous as she could, she didn't break her stride. She circled around the Square before heading out East Main Street. "My life will be even grimmer if I react that way to every Yankee officer I encounter," she muttered under her breath, angry over the shadow of insecurity that seemed to trail her wherever she went.

***

Wednesday was the day of the week Carrie gathered with her friends to read. They called themselves The Circle, the name left over from when they met to sew garments for their men in the Confederate army. The Circle wasn't so big anymore, four, five, or six at the most. Girls from outlying farms had trouble getting past the Yankee pickets, and others had fled with their families after the battle to escape the yoke of another Federal occupation. Perhaps the readers should call themselves The Remnant, one had suggested.

They'd all been unyielding in their support of the Southern cause, but two full months after witnessing the unmitigated horror of a major battle, widening cracks were eroding their solidarity. They'd seen and touched men whose forms were mangled and disfigured in ways they didn't know were possible. Zeal was waning for some, but not all of them.

"If it wasn't for this dreadful war, I'd have my Jim home and we'd be like we used to be," said one of the married ones recently. "I just want it over," said another. "That's so disloyal!" responded another. "We must keep up the fight at all costs!" And another: "There can only be peace on just and honorable terms; death before surrender!"

***

The Circle was gathering at the East Main Street family home of Martha Tidwell Blaylock, the widow of Carrie's brother, Travis. Carrie arrived early, as was her habit, for some time alone with her sister-in-law, who'd evolved into Carrie's most intimate friend besides Lizzy Forbes. The two of them settled in the parlor in front of a popping fire built of green wood.

"How was it?" Martha asked.

"Nashville's a mess. I hardly recognized it."

"As bad as Murfreesboro?"

"Maybe even worse."

Martha listened intently as Carrie related details of her trip: the attack on the train, the hitch over her pass, Lizzy's work as a hospital matron, and her lingering fear over being arrested for smuggling the fabric, flour, and greenbacks.

"Encountering that general sounds like a stroke of incredibly good luck," Martha said.

"I hope you won't think ill of me, but he's not the only Yankee officer I met."

"Think ill of you?"

"Lizzy has a beau, an army surgeon, and I spent some time socializing with them."

"Why would I think ill of you for that?"

"There's more. She was just trying to be nice; she thinks I'm lonely. Maybe I am. Anyway, she arranged for an unmarried officer to come to dinner."

"So?"

"I let him take me to a concert."

Martha turned to the fire with a vacant stare.

"Me, Martha, who's lost a brother to these men, and my future husband, out on the town with one. I must say that I was shocked when he invited me."

Martha sat quietly a little longer, and then looked back at Carrie. "You shouldn't be."

"Shouldn't be?"

"Carrie, wake up."

"Wake up?"

"You, you're an appealing woman."

***

Home alone the following Sunday, Carrie relaxed into a rocking chair on the sunny side of the porch and savored the first hints of spring: insects humming around the rose bushes, birds singing and tweeting, the aroma of warming damp soil, the pregnant buds of the fruit trees, and the yellow daffodils up against the house. No matter how much man's cruelty interfered, the rhythm of life in God's creation continued.

An impulse to add some color to her life had taken hold of her, and after finishing her morning kitchen chores, she'd shed her dreary homespun dress in favor of a printed calico and adorned it with a bright blue scarf around her neck.

Within a minute of opening her book on the porch, her head drooped forward, her chin resting on her chest. It had been another difficult night.

She'd awakened late in the night or early in the morning—she couldn't tell which—with ice cold hands. The sensation took her back more than a year to when they had brought her brother, Travis, home from a fight on the Kentucky border. She'd dipped a washcloth in cold water, wrung it out, and gently wiped it over his feverish face and neck as he drifted in and out of consciousness. Martha had stood by with their baby at her breast watching life slowly bleed out of her husband of less than two years.

On nights when she had trouble getting back to sleep, the flickering light of a bedside candle was enough to allow Carrie to read comforting passages of Scripture. She'd read a passage over and over until sleep returned. Last night it was from Psalm 46.

God is our refuge and strength, a very present help in trouble.
Therefore we will not fear, though the earth be removed, and though the mountains be carried into the midst of the sea.

***

"What's that?" She jerked her head up and spotted the gauzy image of a rider approaching through the orchard. She was unsure if it was a dream until the scabbard of his officer's saber glistening in the midday sun startled her into alertness. "Oh no," she blurted, feeling her pulse quicken and a hint of anger arise; don't these people have anything better to do than harass defenseless women whose only crime is buying flour to bake bread and biscuits and the desire to sleep again between bed sheets?

The hammering in her chest reminded her of the locomotive that brought her back from Nashville. As the man drew up and dismounted, she saw enough of his face beneath his wide-brimmed hat to detect that he was clean-shaven. So it wasn't the provost marshal officer who'd issued the pass for her trip. That man, Goodman, wore a long droopy mustache. Carrie strained to recall the menacing officer at the depot, but she couldn't remember what he looked like.

"Good afternoon."

"Good afternoon," she croaked.

"Are you the lady who recently returned by train from Nashville?"

Her mouth went dry from fright. "I am."

He led his horse to the hitching post and then came back on foot.

"May I join you?" His tone was surprisingly polite.

"Do I have any choice?"

"Indeed you do, madam."

"Well, then have a seat." He seems so young, she thought, but then they all do.

He dragged one of the rockers toward her and removed his hat. His sandy hair, about the color of hers, was parted on the left side.

He's a pleasant-enough looking fellow, she thought, and if I'm going to be arrested, I'd just as soon be taken in by a man who's nice-looking. Why on earth would I have a silly thought like that at a time like this? Heat rose in her cheeks.

"What are you reading?"

"Reading?"

"Your book."

"Oh." She lifted it. "Wordsworth."

"One of my favorite English poets."

It took her a few seconds to be able to say anything. "So you're a literate man?"

"Reading's one of my passions."

Just as it had with General Bradley on the train, talk of books and reading released anxiety's grip on her, if only slightly.

"I shouldn't think a man in your position has much time to read."

He laughed and gave a slight grin. "We've too much time on our hands."

"There's always a throng of people when I go by your office," said Carrie, recalling the jostling she had to absorb when she obtained her pass.

"My office?"

"The provost marshal's office uptown."

"I believe you've mistaken me for someone else. I'm not on the provost marshal's staff."

"You're not?"

"No, ma'am, I'm not."

"Then who are you, and what do you want with me?"

"I'm a captain in the United States Army as you can see, and I've come to question you."

"Question me about what?"

The captain turned his head and gazed off in the distance with a blank stare. It seemed like as much as a half a minute before he uttered a word.

"Pigs."

Carrie clamped her hand over her mouth to try to keep from laughing but couldn't contain it.

"This may not be the most dignified assignment, Miss Blaylock," said the captain, keeping his gaze away from her, "and one that might not advance the cause we both support, but our brief time together will be more agreeable if you wouldn't poke fun at me."

"Cause we both support?"

"Preserving our national Union."

"Oh, yes. I didn't mean any offense, Captain, it's just that I was afraid you're a …" With hardly a thought, she reached for his arm. "You must be the officer who visited a while back. Mother and Sarah said a man had been by. I didn't realize it was you."

She observed his face brighten as he turned it back to face her.

"Your mother said I could catch you here on a Sunday."

She snatched away her hand, slightly alarmed by the breach of decorum. "So you're on General Bradley's staff?"

"I am."

"I've met the general."

"You have? Where?"

"On the cars going to Nashville. I told him about our pigs."

"So that explains it. Well then, tell me what happened."

"It was a Sunday, like today. I was coming back from the … I was away from the house, and when I returned, I saw some soldiers in our pig pen. I yelled, 'Get out of there.' They looked up but paid me no attention. One was a corporal, and I ran up to him. 'Stop it,' I said. 'Those are our only pigs.' He just stared at me. 'Go ahead and take them pigs, boys, these folks are surely secesh.' That's what he said to the men. I pleaded. 'Please corporal, don't take our pigs.' He didn't say anything, and I said: 'You're nothing but common thieves, a disgrace to Abe Lincoln's army.' And he said, 'Little lady, if you don't shut your mouth, I'll lock you up in that there smokehouse of yorn.' That's about all there was to it. They walked off with our squealing pigs and left me in tears."

"You could have told them you're loyal, but then, we often hear that." He asked if there was anything that gave her a clue about their regiment. When she mentioned the corporal's accent and General Bradley's suspicion that they were from Kentucky, the captain reminded her that both armies, Union and Confederate, had regiments from Kentucky and explained that there was one in his brigade.

"Honestly, Captain, we don't care who they are or what brigade they're in. We just want our pigs back."

"Ma'am, there are more than 50,000 soldiers here now and new regiments coming in every day. It would be difficult in the extreme to find those pigs."

"We have no attachment to those particular pigs Captain … I'm sorry, I didn't catch your name."

"John Lockridge."

"Perhaps, Captain Lockridge, you could find us three other pigs."

"I can't make any promises." He asked if she had anything else she wanted to say before he returned to camp.

"Nothing," she replied before she caught herself. "Wait. There is something. You made a favorable impression on my mother."

"The feeling's mutual. She's a dignified and graceful lady."

"I'll pass on the compliment."

"Thank you."

"I believe she told me you're from Ohio. Cincinnati?"

"Columbus."

"Oh yes, the state capital."

"I don't suppose you've ever been there."

Carrie related that the only extensive traveling she'd ever done was when her father took the whole family back to Philadelphia for a visit before the war broke out. They'd spent several nights along the way, including one in Washington City.

He hadn't been much of anywhere, he told her, only some trips to the Finger Lakes region of New York to visit his father's family. "I've seen lots of Tennessee and Kentucky in the last year and a half, which I'm sure I'd like under different circumstances. I do love the green hills and valleys. It reminds me of where I attended college. Although …" The captain paused.

"Although what?"

"I can't say I like everything I've seen down here, if you know what I mean."

"I do, but I avoid political discussions." Carrie shifted in her chair. "So you're the son of an Episcopal clergyman."

"As I believe you are. Ah, the daughter that is."

"Yes, though Father's no longer with us."

"Your mother did tell me that. As I recall, he passed not too long before the war started."

"Two years ago this very month."

Neither of them spoke for a good half-minute.

"Which have you been reading?" he asked.

"Reading?"

"The poems."

"Oh yes, I hadn't really started. There are so many of his I like. I was thinking about 'Lines Composed a Few Miles above Tintern Abbey.' It's tranquil and restorative."

"Could I see it?"

He looked at the contents of the book and then turned to a poem. "I've read that one, and you're right, it is a good one during these times. How about this one, 'Lines Written in Early Spring?' It seems to fit this pleasant day."

"Read it," she said.

The captain looked at the book.

"I mean out loud."

> *"I heard a thousand blended notes,*
> *While in a grove I sate reclined,*
> *In that sweet mood when pleasant thoughts*
> *Bring sad thoughts to mind.*

"That's the first verse," he said, looking into Carrie's eyes.

"Read on, Captain, it's one of my favorites, too."

> *"Have I not reason to lament*
> *What man has made of man?"*

They sat in silence after he read those last lines. Carrie finally spoke up. "How appropriate. I wonder if Wordsworth could have envisioned the devastation we find ourselves in now."

"I hadn't thought of that aspect of it. I just like the way he captures the experience of spring. I'm something of a nature enthusiast." He returned the book to her. "Will you read 'Lines Composed above Tintern Abbey?' It has a springtime theme, too."

"It's quite long."

"I have nothing better … ah, I have no urgent need to return to camp."

"I'll just read a few lines, how about that?" She read out loud, and then they were quiet again.

"That's lovely, Miss Blaylock. You have a nice voice. Do you sing?"

"Thank you, but I'm not musical."

He paused. "This has been most enjoyable, but I don't feel that I should impose upon you any longer. I've obtained the information I came for."

"Information?"

"About the theft of your three pigs."

"Oh, yes. It has been pleasant, Captain, and thank you for your courtesy."

He rose, replaced his hat, went for his horse, and returned mounted in front of the porch.

"Good day, Miss Blaylock," he said, touching the brim of his hat. "Please give my regards to your mother and sister."

After he disappeared into the cedars, she glanced at her hand. It still tingled from the touch of his wool uniform.

***

"So, Lockridge," First Lieutenant Marshall asked that night, "what service did you render today on behalf of our precious Union?"

The captain lay on his cot in the dim light reading the latest letter from his fiancée. It was a full ten seconds before he replied. "I returned to the widow's."

"I'm sure Honest Abe would be grateful for your quest to protect the pork of Tennessee's loyal citizens, if indeed these folks are loyal, which I doubt."

"Don't breathe a word of this to anyone, Marshall; I'll never live it down."

"Well look at the bright side, Lockridge. You got to meet the charming widow and her pretty daughter." They were quiet for a few seconds before the lieutenant spoke again. "Did you meet the older girl? Isn't that why you went back?"

"I interviewed her."

"Did you unearth any clues?"

"Actually I did. But enough of this poking fun, or should I say 'porking' fun," the captain said with a laugh before returning to his letter.

"Well then, Lockridge, let's turn to a more conventional topic for soldiers. Was the older daughter pretty?"

"Not like the other girl, no. She's rather plain-looking. But she's . . ."

"She's what?"

"She's quite intelligent."

***

Carrie's trip to Nashville had been the principal conversation topic at the last gathering of The Circle. She'd shared about conditions in the crowded, filthy city: the food shortages, the horribly high prices for what little there was to buy, and the hatred of the chief army detective, William Truesdail, by loyalists and secessionists alike. It felt a little deceitful, but other than telling the girls about Lizzy and

Gunter, Carrie was careful not to mention meeting the other Federal officers and felt safe that her secret about Major Hobson was secure with Martha.

"I suppose you've heard about Nadine Cothran," said Cat Bonds during a pause in the conversation.

"What about Nadine Cothran?" Ruth Davis asked.

"She's been letting a Yankee call on her," Kate Ellis said.

"It literally makes me sick to my stomach," Cat added.

No one said anything for a few seconds before Gin Conner spoke up. "It makes perfect sense, to me at least."

"Perfect sense? That's outrageous," Cat said.

"That's easy for you to say, Cat, you have a husband," Gin said.

"Well if I didn't, I sure wouldn't go traipsing through a Yankee army camp looking for one."

"She didn't go traipsing through an army camp. They met at a prayer meeting."

"How do you know that?" Kate asked.

"She told me," Gin answered.

"So you've been letting her confide in you? You should be ashamed!"

"Speak for yourself. I'm not ashamed to be loyal to my friends."

"Please, girls, please, this war's hard enough without fighting among ourselves," Martha interjected.

Carrie chimed in. "I'm growing weary of discussing men, the absence of men, and Yankees."

"So you're saying it doesn't matter, is that what you're saying, Carrie?" Cat asked.

"Not to me it doesn't," Carrie shot back.

Olivia Hardison spoke up. "I agree with Carrie. Look at us huddled in this room because we can't lead normal lives. Martha's lost her husband; Carrie's lost her intended; and your husband, Cat, is thirty miles away stuck in some filthy Rebel army camp rife with dysentery and pneumonia leaving you with two small children. Whether Nadine Cothran lets some nameless Federal officer call on her is of no consequence to me, and I say it shouldn't be to any of us. We've got more important things to be concerned about."

"I'll second that," Martha said.

Edith Conley, the quietest of the group, spoke up: "Can't we just read?"

"Yes we can," said Carrie, opening the book resting on her lap. "*The Life and Adventures of Martin Chuzzlewit.*"

"Who's it by?" Kate asked.

"Dickens."

"Not again," said Ruth. "He's so dark."

"Hold on girls," said Martha. She pointed out that when they started their reading circle, they agreed to accept without question the selection of whosever turn it was to make the choice. "Carrie went to a lot of trouble to bring books from Nashville," Martha added.

"From what I know, this one's a bit lighter," Carrie said.

A fragile harmony settled over the gathering as Carrie began reading, but tension lingered.

***

Carrie left The Circle walking with Olivia Hardison toward the Square. "Can I speak to you in strictest confidence?" Olivia asked.

"Of course," Carrie said. "About what?"

"Elton Stephenson."

Reverend Elton Stephenson, pastor of one of the largest churches in town, had suffered a tragedy the summer before when his wife fell victim to a fever that was going around, leaving him with two young boys to raise. The minister, in his mid-thirties, was one of the most respected men in Murfreesboro, and Carrie couldn't imagine what might have transpired between him and Olivia that she needed to keep secret.

"He's asked me to marry him."

Carrie stopped dead in her tracks. "Marry you? I had no idea."

"I didn't either." Glancing around to ensure that no one was listening, Olivia recounted that, along with other women, she took meals for him and his boys now and then. She'd often linger to chat with him, and the last time, she'd stayed and had dinner with the three of them. As she was preparing to leave Elton's house, he'd taken her aside, clasped her hands, and proposed to her.

"What are your feelings about it?" Carrie asked.

"I'm definitely considering it, and I was hoping you could help me think it through." Olivia paused for a second and looked around again. "You're so good at figuring out things."

"Oh, Olivia, I'm not the one you should ask. Several of our friends are married. Ask one of them. Martha is very wise."

"But you had to decide about Grantland."

Carrie hesitated. She'd concluded that she'd been headed to the altar because it was expected of her, but she didn't see how she could share that with Olivia.

"Do you find fault with Elton?" Olivia asked when Carrie didn't respond.

"Oh no, he's a fine man, but …"

"It's his age, isn't it?"

"That crossed my mind."

"And his boys."

"That too."

"Do you think maybe he's just looking for a mistress for his household, someone to mother his boys?"

Lizzy Forbes popped into Carrie's mind. "I'm sure it's a factor, Olivia, how could it not be?"

They resumed walking toward the Square.

"Do you think girls should marry for love? Some think it's a mistake, you know."

"I know they do," Carrie said.

"They say a woman who marries for love is destined for heartbreak. Did you love Grantland?"

"I never thought about it in those terms."

"But you have since his passing."

"You can tell?"

"You may be smarter and calmer than most of us, but you can't hide your feelings, Carrie. And that's why I wanted your advice; you've thought about these things." They stopped again, both glancing around to ensure their privacy. "What else besides love would you look for in a husband?" Olivia asked.

"An education would be high on my list. I'd want a man who enjoys some of the same pursuits I enjoy. And I'd want some degree of autonomy. I'm not going to let any man be my lord and master." Carrie laughed again. "I'd want someone who'll let me argue with him as an equal."

"Kind and considerate?"

"Certainly."

"Faithful to you?"

"That goes without saying."

"See, Carrie, you have thought about these things, and that's exactly why you're the one I wanted to talk to."

"Well, there you have it. But Olivia, what's right for me is not necessarily right for you. I'm sure you'd have a happy life with Elton. And honestly, whether he loves you now, he will. You're a wonderful person."

"Thank you, Carrie, that means a lot, especially coming from you."

***

Nashville
March 9, '63

Dear Carrie,

It was nice to receive your kind thank-you, and Mama and Papa appreciated theirs.

Oh Carrie, being together made me even more aware of how I've missed you. I hope I can love someone else as much as I love you. I'm already scheming for us to reunite.

It pleases me that you approve of Gunter. He's not the tall handsome man girls dream of, but then plump little me is not exactly the belle of the ball. You know me about as well as anyone, and it's reassuring you believe we're a good match. I don't know what the future holds—does anybody these days?

Be sure to tell your mother again of Papa's offer for your family to come and stay with us. It pains me to think of my best friend living under such dreadful conditions. You're so strong.

Major Hobson asked after you recently and said that he regretted that circumstances at the depot prevented a proper goodbye and asked that I inquire whether you would consent to receive his letters. He does seem to be taken with you. And why wouldn't he be? So, let me know, and I'll pass on your response.

Please give my regards to your mother and Sarah. I think the last time I even saw her was at our graduation almost three yeas ago. Can you believe it?

I must be off to the hospital. Write again soon my dear.

All my love,
Lizzy Forbes

***

Captain Lockridge sat at the table inside the walled tent serving as brigade headquarters finishing his draft of a report for Brigadier General Bradley to send to Major General Negley, the division commander. The brigade had returned from a three-day foraging expedition, or "scout" as it was officially termed, out toward Woodbury. They'd brought in wagons overflowing with fodder and hay they'd "requisitioned."

The impact on the citizenry of these expeditions depended largely on the philosophy of each brigade commander. Some permitted and even encouraged their men to plunder anything they could eat. "We must take what we can use and destroy the rest," another of Negley's brigade leaders said. "The war may never end if we don't. Should the Johnnies return, they'll help themselves to whatever's there, or the local secesh devils will give it to them."

There was some logic to that way of thinking, but Captain Lockridge couldn't get around his belief that it was wrong. It was stealing. General Bradley had said before they marched out of camp that he'd rather fight the Rebs a little longer than know he'd caused helpless children to go to bed hungry.

The men of the brigade took only the fodder and hay General Rosecrans authorized them to take, and left behind written receipts that might someday be redeemed for payment. That may not be much more than a legal fiction, the captain observed, but at least it made him feel like they weren't stealing from poor people who already had hardly anything left.

The captain felt fortunate that a twist of fate had landed him serving under such an upstanding man as Bradley. To assemble his brigade staff, the newly minted brigadier solicited suggestions from regimental commanders. The colonel of the Second Ohio recommended John Lockridge. The captain was blessed with a systematic and organized way of thinking. He paid close attention to details, was steady and dependable under pressure, and possessed a gift for reading and writing—just the kind of man Bradley needed for brigade adjutant. And he shared Bradley's Republican politics, which didn't hurt in an army eaten up with political dissension.

***

Carrie was hemming the new sheets in the parlor with her mother when midday sleepiness overcame her. The night before, it was Grantland who had haunted her. She'd stirred from her sleep speculating whether the gray uniform tunic she'd helped his mother sew had rotted in the steamy pit near the little Shiloh meeting house. Where was his body among the seven hundred Confederates the Yankees heaved into a mass grave?

Lying in the darkness, she recalled her confusion in the days following word of Grantland's death. What did propriety dictate? Should she don the black mourning dress as Martha and others had? She and Grantland weren't even engaged, much less married. At least, she'd thought back then, she wouldn't have to concern herself with how to respond to another man's attention. Grantland was the only boy who'd ever shown even the slightest interest in her.

These nighttime interruptions were becoming more frequent. The week before, Carrie had awakened to the sensation of her father's cold skin on her lips. She recalled kissing his forehead just before they closed the casket. A few nights before, she couldn't shake the shock of discovering that a wide-eyed, wounded boy laying in the female seminary whose face she was washing was dead. Other nights, her sleep was interrupted by visions of the ghastly accumulation of severed arms and legs piled outside the makeshift hospital in their church.

Last night she'd lit the candle, opened her Bible to Psalm 102, and read it and reread it until sleep overtook her.

> *Hear my prayer, O Lord, and let my cry come unto thee.*
>
> *Hide not thy face from me in the day when I am in trouble; incline thine ear unto me: in the day when I call answer me speedily.*

***

Carrie had gone up for a nap after falling asleep sewing. She clutched the banister and drowsily made her way down the stairs from her bedroom. She fully awoke the instant she stepped back into the parlor.

"Good afternoon, Miss Blaylock."

"Oh, Captain." She instinctively held back her hand for an instant before extending it. It was red and raw from her never-ending kitchen work. His hand felt coarse and calloused to her touch.

Carrie joined her mother on the settee and sat lady-like, her feet close together and her hands clasped on her lap. The captain returned to the stuffed chair by the window.

"We're talking about our families," her mother said, glancing at her oldest daughter. She related that after her husband finished his studies at the University of Pennsylvania and they married, he took a position in her family's mercantile business in Philadelphia. He felt a calling to enter the ministry, and following a period of reflection and study, the bishop ordained him. It just so happened that her husband's Uncle Edward, his mother's brother, who lived at the time in this very house, was part of a movement to start an Episcopal church in Murfreesboro. It was already an important town in Tennessee, having once been the capital, and with the region's rich agricultural bounty and the railroad coming, everyone expected it to boom. David Blaylock answered the call, and this had been his only parish.

"Your loyal sympathies are understandable," said the captain, remarking about their coming from Philadelphia.

There was a long silence before Amanda spoke again. "My daughter tells me you love literature. Did you attend a college?"

"I did. Kenyon, in Ohio. Perhaps being of the Episcopal faith, you're acquainted with it."

"It has a fine reputation, particularly for a western institution. And did you begin your legal training right away?"

"Yes. I was called to the bar in sixty and practiced for about a year before the war interrupted."

"I know all about that," she said. "And your fiancée, Captain? Tell me about her."

"We became engaged in January when I was fortunate to be home on furlough. Her name is Miranda Escobar. Her parents came from Spain and eventually migrated to Ohio. By the way, Mrs. Blaylock, you have the look of someone of Mediterranean lineage, if you don't mind me saying so."

"My ancestors were French Huguenots who came to America by the way of the Caribbean. So what else do you like to read?"

"Most anything," he said, "but particularly poetry, and I read what I can about natural sciences." The captain looked at the cases on the wall. "You have a nice collection of books."

The door opened, interrupting the conversation. Sampson carried in an armload of firewood and loaded it in the wooden box in the corner of the room.

"Thank you, Sampson," Amanda Blaylock said. The boy glanced at the captain and walked out.

No one spoke for a few seconds, and Carrie used the pause to study their books. Her mother then spoke up, telling the captain she needed to clarify something so there was no misunderstanding.

"What's that, ma'am?"

"Your assumption that we're Unionists is not entirely accurate."

"Oh?"

"It's true that we're originally from Pennsylvania and that my husband spoke out against secession before his unexpected death. I tried to remain neutral after war broke out, but it wasn't easy. My son, Travis, enlisted with the Confederates. So by your definition, we're Rebels."

"My definition?"

"Your army's definition. When your soldiers come upon property of a family with a son or a husband in the Confederate forces, they consider themselves entitled to walk off with anything they fancy."

"I'm aware of that practice, but I have no first-hand experience with it. Our brigade commander is quite strict."

"Travis was elected a company commander in his infantry regiment and held the rank of captain, like you." She looked past him, out the window. "He was mortally wounded in the fight at Mill Springs just over the Kentucky line, on January 19 of last year."

"Please accept my condolences, Mrs. Blaylock."

"Thank you."

Carrie noticed her mother staring intently at the captain before she spoke.

"My experience is one I hope your mother never suffers."

There was an awkward silence until they heard the front door slamming shut. Sarah Blaylock stood silhouetted in the parlor doorway.

"Oh hello, Captain, I saw the army horse and wondered if it was you."

"Good afternoon, Sarah," he said, rising to greet her.

"Did you bring our pigs?"

"Ah, no, I haven't … ah … been able to locate your pigs."

"Then why did you return to our house?"

"Sarah, there's no need for you to question the captain," Amanda interrupted.

Sarah continued standing in the door facing him.

"That's quite all right, ma'am," he said, glancing at Amanda. "I'm working on it, Sarah, I assure you. I've looked through our brigade's camp, but I haven't seen your pigs. I'm not giving up, though."

She kept her eyes trained on his for a few seconds and then walked away. Her steps up to the second floor echoed from the central hallway.

Carrie expected to see the captain's look of disapproval of her feisty little sister. She saw instead what looked like a spark of attraction.

"Please excuse her, Captain; she tends to be the passionate one in our family."

"No offense taken, ma'am."

***

That night in their hovel, First Lieutenant Marshall folded the latest edition of the *Chicago Tribune* he'd received from his father and set it on the little table holding the oil lamp. "So, Lockridge, what are you reading?"

"Tennyson."

"Where'd you get that?"

"The widow's."

"You went again?"

"Yep."

"Have you reported all this to Bradley?"

"Not yet. He may have forgotten about it."

"Then why keep burdening yourself with this absurd mission?"

I've wondered that myself, thought the captain. Today I may have found the answer. A feeling of emptiness had arisen in him riding up the Salem Pike away from River Bluff Farm. The warmth and cheeriness of the parlor, the shelves of books, and the gentleness of feminine company had nourished him. In fact, he thought, the place feels more like home than my own did when I was there on furlough. True, there had been the joy and relief of the engagement. But still, he'd noticed an unsettled sensation. He'd felt out of place even in his own house. At the widow's, he didn't feel that way.

"It's actually a nice place to visit," he said to the lieutenant. "Helps relieve the boredom of this rotten camp life."

"Did you just help yourself to the book?"

"They loaned it to me. As I was riding away from the house, I heard someone calling. I drew up and saw the girl chasing after me. She said she wanted to loan me the Tennyson."

"Which girl, the pretty one?"

"The older one."

***

Captain Lockridge couldn't tell whom it was at first, the widow, one of her girls, or the Negro woman, but when he got close enough to alert whomever it was, Amanda Blaylock stood and turned in his direction. She seemed to be tending to flowers. A good day for it, he thought, a brilliant early spring day. Her effort to keep her house bright with flowers during this dreadful time reinforced his favorable impression of her. He dismounted.

"Good afternoon, Captain. To what do we owe the honor of your visit?"

"To return the book."

"What book?"

"This one." Holding the reins in his left hand, he retrieved the Tennyson from his saddlebag. "Your daughter loaned it to me."

"Which daughter?"

"The older one."

"I'm afraid she's away from the house just now, but you can leave it with me, and I'll see that she gets it."

The captain stared into her handsome face for a few seconds. "This is probably my last visit here, Mrs. Blaylock. With the warmer weather, we'll be moving out any day now. I'd like to return it to her personally."

She looked into his eyes as if studying him. "I don't see any harm in it. She often goes off to read by herself. Follow the path on that side of the house," she said, pointing, "and you'll eventually come to a gazebo on a bluff above the river. You should find her there."

***

The captain made his way along the narrow path, the sleeves of his coat brushing against the boughs of the dark green cedars. He emerged from the evergreen thicket into a rocky open area where he stopped. There were hardly any trees, and instead of grass, the ground was littered with loose gravel, jagged-edged flat rocks, and dormant weeds. A faint path led to the right in the direction of the pike, but the main trail turned sharply left in the direction of the Stones River.

Standing in this eerie setting, the captain was seized by a disquieting notion. He was traipsing through here without a second's thought to his own safety. Bushwhackers managed to penetrate the Union lines now and then, or so it was rumored, and these dense cedar woods would make a good hiding place for desperate deserters to await the cover of darkness. Another unsettling thought crossed his mind. Have I become too trusting of the Widow Blaylock and her daughters?

The path to the river from the open area climbed a slight rise, and when it did, he entered a different world. In place of scrubby cedars and scattered rocks, bulky hardwoods, mostly oak and hickory, stood tall over an understory of budding sugar maple, and last year's tan beach leaves clung tenuously to the branches. Off to his left rose a jumble of small boulders, about waist high, covered in a rich green moss that made him think of velvet pillows.

After a few more steps he heard the sound of the river, and after a few more he saw the forest open up ahead. His mind shot back to the faint path coming from the pike. It's there for a reason, he thought. And he recalled the widow's emphatic words on his first visit: *She has no husband.* There may be someone with the girl, possibly a man her mother doesn't know about.

The noise of the river would mute the sound of his footsteps shuffling through the forest duff, so he left the path and treaded carefully off to the right through the hardwoods until he came to the river. He crept upstream from tree to tree until he neared the clearing. Peeking from behind the flaking bark of a fat sycamore, he studied the gazebo.

It was an eight-sided affair with a cedar shake roof. A rail and a sitting bench ran around seven of the sides with the eighth left open for the entrance. Vertical pickets connected the rail, the bench, and the floor. Most of the whitewash was gone, exposing the red cedar. Carrie Blaylock sat on the section of the bench opposite the opening, her head tilted down. He patiently studied the area for at least a minute to satisfy himself no one was with her before emerging from the woods.

"Oh!" she gasped. "Where did you come from?"

"I'm sorry if I startled you."

He was startled, too, by her appearance. The girl's face was barely visible beneath a big bonnet, the type farm women wear in the fields. She wore a dull gray dress made of rough homespun with blotches of what looked like blood stains on the front. He did a double take when he saw her feet; she wore men's Wellington boots. She didn't look much different from the pitiful refugees he'd seen aimlessly wandering the roadsides seeking reprieve from the clutches of war.

They looked at each other for an awkward instant without speaking.

"What brings you here?" she asked.

The tremble in her voice made him wonder if she was expecting someone. "To return the Tennyson." He held up the book.

"That's thoughtful of you."

They looked at each other without speaking for another few seconds. "Well, here it is." He walked into the gazebo, handed it to her, and returned to the entrance.

"Did you get a chance to read any of it?" she asked, showing a slight smile.

"I read all of it."

"I hope you liked it."

"I did."

There was another pause. "What are you reading?" he asked.

She looked down at the open book on her lap. "My Bible."

He glanced around before looking back at her. "Any part in particular?"

"Not really. I mostly just pick it up and find something that strikes me."

He looked away again. "Same here."

"'Same here' what?"

"I mostly pick up my Bible and read what strikes me." He looked at the river flowing swiftly up to the bluff and then back at her.

"Lately I've been reading Psalms," she said.

Neither of them spoke for what seemed to the captain like a long time. "Nice day isn't it?" he finally said.

"Yes, it is a nice day."

He looked back at the river. "The river has a nice flow."

"Not too high, not too low."

"I like it like this."

"Me too."

He turned back to face her. "I suppose I should be going. Thank you for loaning me the book."

"I imagine you have a lot to do."

He stopped just outside the gazebo entrance. "To tell you the truth, Miss Blaylock, it's insufferably boring just hanging around camp all day. Goodbye."

He headed for the path into the hardwoods. Just as he reached the forest edge, he heard her voice.

"Captain?"

He looked back at her. She'd taken off her bonnet.

"What is it Miss Blaylock?"

"Since you're not rushed, why don't you sit for a bit?"

I guess nobody's coming after all, he thought.

***

He couldn't say how long he'd remained at the bluff, but it was long enough for the songs of the spring peepers to fill the air as they do this time of the year when the sun starts dropping behind the trees.

They'd spent much of their time sharing stories about being ministers' children. When they speculated whether their

fathers knew of each other, he promised to ask in his next letter home, though he couldn't guarantee he'd still be around when the reply reached him.

They'd spent the rest of their time swapping information about their favorite authors and poets and about passages of Scripture they found comforting. They took turns reading aloud as they did on the Sunday they first met, only this day it was from the Book of Psalms.

It's amazing, he thought, lying on his cot beneath the canvas roof of his hovel, holding his fiancée's latest letter. What are the odds of meeting up with another child of an Episcopal minister down here in Tennessee and on top of that, a bookworm like me? And nature, she's interested in nature as well. When he'd shared with her his practice of keeping a notebook about the birds he identified around Columbus, she suggested that he do the same in Middle Tennessee, only not just about birds, but whatever in nature he saw. Like Lewis and Clark, she'd laughed, and offered to help him identify things.

Trouble was, now that he'd returned the book and obtained all the facts about the pig theft and reported them to the general, he didn't have any reason to go back to the Blaylocks'.

He'd debated whether to even return the Tennyson. Like the Widow Blaylock had said, General Rosecrans had decreed that any family with men serving with the Johnnies was considered Rebel, and that went for families whose men had lost their lives. But the prospect of a visit to the Blaylocks' inviting parlor and the company of the widow and her daughters had pushed him over the edge, so he'd decided to return it. And besides, it was a nice day for a ride out of the stinking brigade camp.

***

Camp, M'boro, Tenn.
March 24, '63

Buenos Noches Mi Miranda,

Life is still dull in camp, at least for our brigade. The men continue to work on building the big fort. There's talk that we'll go out on another scout, but nothing definite. I did, though, have an out-of-the-ordinary experience. My degrading assignment took me back to the widow's where I was treated to a visit to a quiet and peaceful spot. It's a gazebo crowning a bluff over the Stones River. The bluff's not terribly tall, no more than ten feet. The river rushes to it, then abruptly alters course as it crashes against the limestone outcrop.

The place seems to have miraculously escaped the ravages of war, and I momentarily forgot that I'm a soldier, that's how peaceful it is. There is a secret route to the bluff directly from the public road, so I can return there at my leisure without bothering the widow and her family. It should be a beautiful place in the spring, which is starting to bloom down here.

I was there with the girl I interviewed a while back. I haven't had as much contact with these Southern girls as some of our boys, being the faithful fellow that I am, but enough to perceive that this girl's different. Mostly I've seen ones who, by the time they're her age, have 3 or 4 barefoot children running round the cabin, or the "ladies" with their noses up in the air. She's certainly refined and quite literate, but doesn't give off those haughty airs like so many of her class.

She goes by her maiden name, so I don't think she's been married. But the way her mother had said, "she has no husband" makes me think there's a story there. I wonder if some unkind fellow jilted her. Anyway, that's none of our concern. But I do confess to being curious.

That was my day. What about yours? I trust you're receiving my letters. I so appreciate yours.

I miss you so much, my dear fiancée, and long for the time when we will be united.

With all my love,
John

The captain sealed the envelope, placed it on the battered little table, lay back on his cot, and clasped his hands behind his head. I said I'd write every week, and I'm a man of my word, he thought.

Lying in the stillness of the early spring night, his mind focused on his brief visit home after the battle, on his joy when Miranda Escobar answered yes to his marriage proposal and his relief when her father consented. But images of the tranquil spot above the river kept intruding.

Feeling a chill, he rose from the cot, picked up a piece of stovewood, and laid it on the coals smoldering in the iron stove. An unsettled feeling he couldn't identify plagued him. The sensation, whatever it was, left him only after he took the letter he'd just written, stuffed it into the stove and watched it flare up and disintegrate into a collection of black ashes.

***

Carrie brought breakfast to her mother and sister. The brilliant sun rising in the cloudless morning cast a golden glow over the dining room. On the table she placed a platter holding a few slivers of ham and three eggs she'd scrambled along with a plate of three biscuits.

Amanda spoke as soon as Carrie took her seat. "Let's bow our heads."

We thank thee our Heavenly Father for this food, and we pray that we may be ever mindful of those so near us who don't even have this much to eat. Give us strength, dear God, to make it through another day. We pray for peace. Amen.

"Enjoy these biscuits," said Carrie, passing around the plate. "That's the last of the Nashville flour."

The remark prompted a discussion about not having enough food and the prospect of buying some. The presence for several months of thousands of men who were paid regularly was too much of an opportunity to pass up, and a few stores had reappeared in town. And too, the sutlers, who followed the army, had wagons brimming with food and other merchandise for sale. But the food was beyond the Blaylocks' reach. It was too risky, Amanda explained, to display their money. If word got out that they had greenbacks, they could be preyed upon by the camp followers who arrived in the army's wake or by some of the increasing number of Union army deserters.

"What about that officer who's been here, the one who claims he's trying to find our pigs?" Sarah asked.

"Captain Lockridge?" Amanda said.

"Yes, him. Let's ask him to buy some food for us. We'll give him the money. No one will think anything of him doing it. Maybe we can even invite him to join us."

"Surely you're not getting a crush on that Yankee officer, Little Sister," Carrie said with a grin.

"Well, he is handsome," said Sarah, grinning sideways at Carrie. "And he sure seems to like you."

"Me?"

"I saw how late it was when the two of you returned from the bluff the other day."

"So you've taken to spying on me, have you?"

"Please girls, please," Amanda broke in. "Let's not make something out of nothing. The captain was just returning a book."

"Yes, we did sit out there for a while, and yes, I did enjoy the conversation. He seems like a nice enough fellow. But even if we did want him to help us, I doubt we'll ever see him again. There's no reason for him to come back," said Carrie in a calmer voice.

They silently started consuming the meager meal before Amanda spoke. "As long as the army's here, he'll come back."

***

The assignment intrigued Captain Lockridge. It wasn't that Brigadier General Bradley had given him a written communication to take to a headquarters. That was routine. But the general instructed him to deliver the sealed envelope to the Keeble House, the fine home Major General Rosecrans had appropriated for army headquarters. What was it, the captain wondered, prompting a brigade commander to send a message directly to the army's commanding general, bypassing division and corps? What was it that General Bradley needed to keep to himself? It was speculation, of course, but perhaps General Rosecrans was soliciting confidential evaluations of his division commanders from the brigade commanders serving under them.

The captain was leaving the package with a staff officer when Major General Rosecrans himself appeared. Lockridge had never met the commanding general, and had only laid eyes on him a few times. The general asked who he was and where he was from, and seemed glad to meet another man from Ohio. Their conversation was brief.

As the captain stepped outside, he heard someone call his name. "Captain Lockridge." It was a female voice.

The low morning sun blinded him. Walking toward the sound of the voice, he recognized Sarah Blaylock.

"Hello, Sarah. What brings you here?"

"I'm on my way to my friend Katie Foster's out by the female seminary. You know where that is?"

"It's where they put the wounded Rebs."

They stood for an instant without speaking.

"I'd be pleased to have you escort me there."

He couldn't hide his hesitancy. "But if you don't want to," Sarah continued, "or you don't have time, that's all right."

"I'd like to, but," he said with a smile, "I don't want to ruin the reputation of a fifteen-year-old girl."

"Is there something about you we don't know?" she asked with a mischievous grin.

"No," he laughed. "I mean, just being out on the street with an enemy soldier."

"Oh, I don't care about that kind of stuff anymore."

"Well then let's be on our way," he said, noticing how comfortable he felt with the girl. They walked side-by-side along College Street.

"By the way, Captain, how do you know I'm fifteen?"

"Your sister told me."

They walked on in silence a little farther before Sarah spoke. "You like her, don't you?"

"Who?"

"My sister."

"I like all of you."

"Did she tell you how old she is?"

"Not that I recall."

"She's twenty-one. Mother said people who don't know me think I'm older, more like eighteen or nineteen. She said she had to warn me of that when our army came back in November, as if I can't look out for myself. They're some who think Carrie's older than twenty-one."

"She's an intelligent, articulate, and informed lady."

"It's not that. Everybody in town knows how smart she is."

"Then what do you mean?"

"There are those who think she doesn't like to have fun. Part of it's because she doesn't come to town with us on Sundays anymore, and part of it comes from Mattie Ready's wedding. Do you know about that?"

"No."

"She married General Morgan."

"I did hear about General Morgan's wedding. General Polk officiated, I believe, but I didn't know who he married. Did you go?"

She did, said Sarah, explaining that before the Readys ran off with Bragg's army following the battle, Mattie's sister, Alice, had been one of Sarah's closest friends.

"What does the wedding have to do with people saying Carrie doesn't like to have fun?"

"Carrie didn't go to the wedding," Sarah said. "It was the biggest social event in a long time, and Carrie missed it."

"Why?"

"She was home sick in bed. It wasn't because she didn't want to be sociable." She paused for an instant. "Does she strike you as a stick in the mud?"

"I don't have an opinion about your sister, Sarah, really other than I've enjoyed her company the few times I've seen her. Like I said, I enjoy being with all three of you."

"She's not a stick in the mud, Captain; I want you to know that."

"Well, Sarah, you know, none of this is really any of my business."

"I know something about her no one else does."

"Well, she's your sister."

"It's something I can't even share with Mother."

The captain searched for something to say. "So, she's six years older than you."

Sarah explained that there had been a child between them, a boy, Edward, but that he'd died of the croup at age six months. She told the captain that she wished she had a brother or sister closer to her age. She got lonely sometimes, and that's why she came into town so often to see her friends. They continued walking.

"Can I trust you with a secret?" she said.

"I suppose that depends on what it is. I mean, if you share something useful to our army, I may not be able to keep it secret."

"Oh, nothing like that."

She stopped walking, and he did too. She moved close to him, close enough for the full skirt of her dress to brush against his legs as it had the first time he met her. Sarah glanced around as if to ensure no one was watching, and then leaned into him even further, almost close enough for her breasts to press against him. He had the sudden impulse to wrap his arms around her and kiss her right there in broad daylight, and instantly felt ashamed for the thought.

"We have money."

"We?"

"Our family."

"And?"

"Real money, genuine U.S. greenbacks."

"Why are you telling me this?"

"Because you can help us."

"Help you, how?"

"You can buy things." She took a step back and lifted the skirt of her dress to show off her right foot. "Look."

It felt odd peering at her foot, but he saw what she was talking about. The sole of her shoe had separated from the upper, revealing a filthy stocking in the breach.

"You want me to buy you shoes?"

"No. I just wanted to show you how bad things are. I want you to buy us food."

***

Captain John Lockridge was taking a risk riding out the Woodbury Pike beyond the picket outposts protecting the army's vast encampment around Murfreesboro. Wheeler's Rebel cavalry had been probing the Federal defenses, and if the timing of his solo expedition coincided with a raid in this direction, the war would be over for him. They'd all heard stories about conditions in Southern prisons, and he'd reached the same conclusion as the rest of the officers: I'd sooner take my chance in battle than in Richmond's Libby

Prison. And if I run into a pack of guerrillas or bushwhackers, he thought, I won't even make it to prison to die.

He recognized the place to turn off the pike, where a creek flowed under a bridge. Making his way up the rough side road, he wondered as he had before how it got its name, Cripple Creek. It's beautiful country, he thought, particularly to a flatlander like me. The creek tumbled out of a narrowing valley enclosed by fingers of a forested highland. The pastures had shed their brown coats for green, and the tender chutes of sugar maple gave the forest edge a fuzzy, red gloss. They sound like they're welcoming me, he said to himself at the singing of the meadowlarks, but he knew that not even birds would welcome a Yankee to this fertile valley.

About a mile from the pike, he turned onto a farm lane and splashed through the creek. He saw the house ahead on the hill. A patch of woods led up the hill to the left, and he turned into it, dismounted, and hitched his horse to a maple sapling. He crept up the hill through the woods, went to the left of the farmhouse, and darted to the edge of the barn where he had a good view of the back of the house and the other outbuildings.

He saw a woman. She was bent over churning butter, it looked like. When she stood up straight and pressed her hand into the small of her back, a flash of fear shot through him. She was with child. He unfastened the holster carrying his pistol. There must be a man around.

The captain heard the shotgun blast and the pregnant woman's scream at the same time he felt buckshot splatter across his backside.

So this is how I'm going to die, he thought, and waited for the shot to tear into his skin.

"Get them hands up in the air, boy."

He couldn't see her, but he recognized the voice. They'd encountered the woman when they were here foraging.

"I can hit squirrel at forty paces, and I surely won't have any trouble hittin' you."

In that split second the captain was aware that dirt had splattered across his back not buckshot. She'd fired a warning shot into the ground.

"Betty Lou, come over here and get this here boy's gun."

He saw when she approached that she wasn't more than a girl. He had the instinct to grab her for a shield, but the image of his sister Miriam with her newborn sparked in his mind. The girl took his weapon and left his sight.

"Turn around, boy, and keep them hands up."

He turned slowly and saw the girl standing next to the woman with a double-barreled shotgun pointed at him.

"I ought to shoot, you damn Yankee. Just give me one reason why I shouldn't shoot you dead."

"I'm here to offer you money."

"Money?"

"Silver dollars."

"You're going pay me for what you boys taken the other day?"

"Not exactly, but I'm prepared to give you U.S. dollars for what I'm here to take today."

"Take today? What are you talking about, boy? We ain't got much left."

"One of those little pigs over there. I'm here to take one and pay you for it."

"You must be crazy."

"I've a pressing need for a little pig, and maybe more if you'll cooperate with me."

"What'll you give me?"

"I'm thinking two dollars?"

"Two dollars for one of them little runts?"

"That's right."

"If some of them boys romping around here stealing and robbing, pretending they're for the Southern cause find out that I sold something to a Yankee, they'll burn me out."

"No one will know but you and me, and the girl there."

"She's my daughter. Her husband's off in the army."

Ah yes, the captain said to himself, remembering that the Confederates came back to this area in mid-November. More than once he'd imagined how pretty his fiancée, Miranda, would look in a family way.

"What are you going to do with a little pig? You can't get two dollars to resell it."

"I have a particular need for a pig."

"Well show me the money then."

"I can't with my hands in the air."

"All right, take 'um down, but don't try nothing smart, or I'll shoot you."

He took the silver dollars from his pocket.

"I'll need your help, lady. I'm a city boy, and not versed in how to transport a pig."

"You tie it up, Captain, tie it up by its legs."

"Do you have a bag big enough to hold the pig while I ride back to town?"

"You sure you're not crazy?"

"I know exactly what I'm doing."

"Throw them dollars on the ground and back up a few paces."

He did as instructed.

"Betty Lou, pick up the money."

The girl picked up the coins and studied them. "They look real, Mama."

"They're real, I assure you," the captain said.

The woman lowered the shotgun and exchanged it with her daughter for the dollars. The girl put his revolver on the ground.

"You wait right here, boy. Betty Lou, shoot him if he tries anything."

"Don't worry, Mama."

The woman walked into the barn and came out in a few seconds with a big cloth sack, the kind that holds seed, and a length of rope. The captain watched as she went to the pigpen, captured a squealing creature, bound its legs, and stuffed it in the bag. She presented the bag with the pig wiggling inside.

"Here boy, now don't you breathe a word of this, you hear?"

"I give you my word."

"A Yankee's word ain't worth much, but it's all I got. Now you get out of here before I change my mind and shoot you."

John picked up his revolver and walked back toward his horse with the pig kicking inside the bag.

CHAPTER FOUR
April 1863

John Lockridge was the type who followed the rules. As a schoolboy, as a student at Kenyon College, as a promising young lawyer, and now as a volunteer army officer, he was intentional about staying within the boundaries of propriety and integrity he set for himself. As far as he was concerned, it was an outdated practice left over from when women were considered property of their fathers or husbands, but he had followed the rule by asking Miranda Escobar's father's permission to marry his daughter.

So the captain needed to reassure himself that he wasn't breaking the rules each time he rode away from the army camp to visit the Blaylocks'. Making out the detail for the guard, transmitting to the regiments orders from division headquarters, and assisting Brigadier General Bradley with his reports rarely occupied the brigade adjutant for more than a few hours. And hadn't the general given tacit permission to leave when he groused about how dull it was during the endless wait for the next campaign. "I have hardly enough to do to keep me awake," the brigadier had said one day to his assembled staff.

Still, the captain felt the tug of his conscience whenever he made the short ride to River Bluff Farm. But not enough of a tug to restrain himself. And he wasn't about to pass on the Widow Blaylock's invitation to join them for dinner the Saturday before Easter.

***

"That's the best meal I've had since … I can't remember," the captain said.

"Since you were home on furlough? I'm sure your mother fixed you something special," said Amanda, flashing a mother's smile.

The captain chuckled. "Truthfully, Mrs. Blaylock, this seems better."

"Please, don't ever tell your mother that," she said, still smiling.

"You're to be congratulated."

"It was my daughter here," said Amanda, nodding to Carrie. "She's the cook these days."

Carrie had prepared a one-dish meal in the Dutch oven. She took the fresh beef that Captain Lockridge bought, gave some to Cassie, and carved the remainder into bite-sized chunks. She diced carrots, potatoes, turnips, and onions retrieved from the root cellar and put them with the beef into a roux made with some of the flour and salt he bought for them. The biscuit crust came out golden and flaky, just as she'd hoped.

"My congratulations, Miss Blaylock," the captain said, looking at Carrie.

"It's really nothing," replied Carrie, feeling a sudden whisk of anger for her false modesty. She was actually quite proud of it.

"There's more; we have dessert," Amanda said.

"Really, Mrs. Blaylock, I don't deserve this. After all, I've only returned one pig."

Amanda's face lit up again. "It's nice for us to have you here, Captain Lockridge. I hope you know you're welcome anytime."

Carrie left for the kitchen and returned with bowls of a steaming crisp she'd baked with dried apples, cornmeal, molasses, and eggs.

"I don't have a name for this. It's just something I concocted. I hope it's edible."

Carrie blushed at the captain's response. "If you fixed it, Miss Blaylock, it's bound to be good."

***

Trinity Episcopal Church wasn't one of the larger ones in Murfreesboro, and it could barely accommodate the Easter crowd. The dwindling congregation had been meeting in private homes where one of the men would read Morning Prayer, and they would have to resume that practice. Major General William S. Rosecrans made it clear when he gave permission to use the church that it was a one-time event. The sick and wounded would be returned before sundown.

Amanda Blaylock at first resisted the urgings of her fellow parishioners to seek the general's permission. It's irritating, she'd thought, how some of the very people who pleaded with her were the ones she suspected of talking behind her back about her questionable loyalty. But when it was convenient for them to embrace her Northern origin, they showed no hesitation. In the end she decided she'd ask because more than any of them, she wanted to worship in the church where her husband had been its only minister.

So she dressed in the most dignified outfit she could assemble, marched into the Keeble House, and asked to see General Rosecrans. For all she knew, some impudent young staff officer would laugh her out of headquarters. But the general saw her and was courteous to the point of seeming solicitous. He spent the better part of an hour alone with her.

Word of the service spread through some of the camps, and a healthy contingent of mostly officers squeezed into the church. Everyone stood. The pews had long before been dragged out and chopped up for firewood.

***

Captain Lockridge didn't see the Blaylocks during the service, but later he spotted the widow in the crowd mingling outside. He picked his way to her and again expressed his gratitude for the dinner and for informing him about the service.

"We're glad to bring a little brightness into the life of a soldier so far from those who love him," she said.

"Are your girls here?"

"There's Sarah over there."

He looked in her direction. The girl was staring sideways at him. When their eyes met, she gave him a hidden wave with the tips of her fingers.

"I don't see Carrie," said Mrs. Blaylock, tilting her head to look over the crowd. "Ah, there she is, talking to Olivia Hardison and … I don't know that man."

He wouldn't have recognized Carrie. She wore a navy blue dress fringed with a white collar, a burgundy jacket open in the front, and a fashionable hat the same color as her jacket. Her hair was up in the back, revealing the curve of her slender neck. He'd never thought of her that way, but she looked pretty. A quiver of guilt ran through him, but then again, he thought, there's no rule that a committed man can't at least notice an attractive woman.

She was talking to another young woman and to an older man who was missing his right arm. His empty sleeve was stuffed into his coat pocket. She excused herself and joined the captain and her mother. After exchanging greetings, the captain offered to escort the three of them back to the farm.

"We're heading over to the Tidwell's, the family my son Travis married into," Mrs. Blaylock said. "Presbyterians they are, so they're not here. I usually spend Sunday afternoons with them." She broke into a broad smile. "And with my grandson, David; he does love his Granny Mandy."

"I'll be on my way then." He turned to Carrie. "Thank you again for such a nice dinner, Miss Blaylock."

"It was my pleasure, Captain, and thank you for assisting us," she said with a countenance that warmed his insides.

"We should work in more dinners while we still have the opportunity," Amanda said.

"All you need to do is ask, and that goes for helping with the purchases as well."

***

Carrie had stewed about Major Hobson ever since Lizzy's letter. She wanted to exchange letters with the man. He was witty and engaging in person, and she assumed he would be in his correspondence as well. And he was so kind to her. But if she said yes, he'd interpret it as being open to a courtship. That was out of the question, no matter how much she liked him.

So the Wednesday after Easter she stopped by the post office on her way to The Circle and mailed her reply. She instructed Lizzy to politely tell the major no and to express again her gratitude for his assistance. Given his duties as assistant departmental quartermaster, there was always the possibility that he'd show up in Murfreesboro and seek her out. He didn't strike her as a man who'd easily give up. I'll just have to cross that bridge when I come to it, she thought.

***

A week had passed since she'd mailed the letter about Major Hobson, and Carrie arrived at The Circle gathering early as usual to spend a few minutes with her sister-in-law.

"Carrie, what do you know about that Federal officer who's been coming by your farm?" Martha asked.

"He's from Ohio, an Episcopal minister's son."

"What else do you know?"

"Why do you ask?"

"Your mother seems to mention him every time I see her."

"Let's see," Carrie said. "He's a lawyer, he's twenty-five."

"Sounds familiar, doesn't it?"

"That's crossed my mind, the similarities with Travis."

"I can't imagine losing my son, and I don't see how she holds up so well." Martha paused. "This is a sensitive topic, but do you think she's trying to replace Travis? Am I awful for even thinking such a thing?"

"If you are, so am I. It's occurred to me as well."

"Do you care that people might try to make something of it?"

"I doubt many even know about him. And besides, the army will be marching away any day now that spring has arrived."

"There was talk of it after Easter church," Martha said haltingly.

"By who?"

"I promised not to say. I mention it just to point out that it has been noticed."

"Did your source tell you that I was talking to him after church too?" asked Carrie, with a hint of irritation.

"Actually, yes."

"There's no cause for anyone to think a thing about it."

There was a knock on the door, and as Martha went to it, Carrie grabbed her arm. "Sister, don't say anything about the captain coming to our place. You know how Cat goes off."

"Don't worry."

***

The gathering started with the usual exchanges of gossip and rumors posing as war news.

"Carrie, who was that man you were talking to after Easter church?" Gin Conner asked.

"He is a …"

"My cousin," Olivia broke in.

"Oh, him," Carrie said. "Remind me of his name, Olivia?"

"Morton Walling."

"Yes, Morton Walling."

"I've never seen a cousin of yours around here," Cat Bonds said.

"He's not from around here," Olivia said.

"From Alabama," Carrie injected.

"What's he doing here?" Kate Ellis asked.

"He was wounded in the battle, on the third day, and left for dead. The Yankees took him to one of those dreadful Nashville hospitals they set aside for our boys. They paroled him when he was well enough to travel, and he came to Murfreesboro. He has a daughter back in Alabama and he's trying to figure out how to get her."

"What happened to his wife, the girl's mother?" someone asked.

Olivia looked down. "She passed early in the war—typhoid fever. The girl's living with the grandparents on her mother's side."

Gin Conner spoke up: "Carrie, I heard you were talking to a Yankee officer after church."

"Yes. A young man from Ohio. He's been to our place several times.

"Not causing you any trouble I hope," Cat said.

Martha broke in. "I understand he's quite nice, a gentleman who's been helpful to her mother."

"Well surely there must be a few gentlemen. After all, it's a big army," Kate said. "Maybe not many, but a few."

Everyone laughed.

"I heard he's handsome," Gin said.

"Who told you that?" Carrie asked.

"I'm not saying."

Everyone laughed again, including Carrie. "I suppose he is," she said. And so is Olivia's cousin, she thought, but in a different way.

***

Carrie lingered after the others left.

"You know, Martha, I've thought about another aspect of Mother and the captain."

"And?"

"Safety. Both times our place was invaded, he would have outranked any of those Yankees." Carrie recounted how the first time, a smart-aleck lieutenant had led the Federal soldiers. His men rifled through the entire house searching for meat, but hadn't found it. Sampson had cut a trap door in the ceiling above the second floor that was impossible to detect, and they'd stashed in the attic their hams and bacon. The next time with the pigs, a corporal was in charge.

"Take advantage of his presence while you can," Martha said. "I'm hearing every day how Lincoln is pressuring Rosecrans to move toward Chattanooga."

***

When Captain Lockridge satisfied himself no one had followed him off the Salem Pike, he tethered his horse to an immature beech tree, retrieved the leather valise from his saddlebag, and picked his way along the little path to the rocky forest opening.

Tucked into his valise were the notebook and pencil he'd bought from a sutler, the latest letter from his fiancée, stationery, and pen and ink. Undisturbed by the tumult of war and soothed by the sound of the river rippling past the bluff, he hoped to convey to Miranda the peace and serenity of the spot.

The gazebo clearing had been freed from winter's grip and was bordered now by pink clusters of blooming redbud. It's hard to believe, he thought, taking his seat on the bench; this place has stayed so pure, so unspoiled. The young officer laid out his stationery next to his pen and ink bottle, and leaned back, spreading his arms along the rail. Allowing his eyes to sink shut, he absorbed the sounds and aromas of the fresh Middle Tennessee spring and visualized his fiancée—

her dark brown eyes, her full moist lips, the curve of her hips. He could almost feel her in his arms.

A rustling in the woods startled him. Lowering his right hand to his holster, the image of bushwhackers and deserters flashed across his mind. He turned to see if it was only his imagination. It was the girl.

"Miss Blaylock." He took his hand off his holster.

"I'm surprised to find you here," she said.

He could tell that by the look on her face. As they studied each other, he recalled wondering whether the girl was in the habit of meeting someone, someone she *wouldn't* be surprised to see.

"Perhaps I should leave you alone," she said.

He observed her looking at his writing material. "Ah no, Miss Blaylock, this is after all, your place not mine."

He gazed at her indecisively before standing to face her. "I wonder if you'd do something for me."

"I suppose that depends on what it is."

"Of course." What a stupid way for me to put it, he thought. "You recall our conversation about my nature journal? I bought a notebook, and what I meant was, would you help me identify the flowers blooming in the woods?"

"Are you sure you wouldn't rather be left alone?"

He detected reluctance in her voice. "Quite sure," he said, shading the truth, if only a little.

He slid the stationery, pen, and ink bottle into the valise, took out his notebook and pencil and joined her. She had a book tucked under her arms.

"What's the book?"

"Sir Walter Scott. *Waverley*."

"I hear Scott's particularly popular in the South."

"I just like his books," Carrie replied. "I brought it back from Nashville."

They stood facing each other for a few seconds. "Let's have a look," he said. She followed him into the woods and came to his side when he halted. "These flowers seem to be everywhere," he said, spreading out his left arm.

"We call them spring beauty. They're usually the first to come out, as early as the first or second week of March when we have a normal winter."

"So it's been an unusually cold winter down here?"

"Most certainly."

He took his pencil and wrote in the notebook: "Spring beauty, April 9, Blaylock farm." He pointed to a plant blooming at the base of a hickory.

"That's bloodroot."

"An odd name."

"If you break the stem, it oozes a juice that resembles blood." She knelt and touched the flower's stem. "Let me show you."

"No, no," he said, laying his hand on her shoulder.

When she looked up at him, he pulled away his hand, and observed a puzzled expression on her face.

"It's just that … well … I've seen enough blood lately to last a lifetime."

As he made the record in his notebook, she stood up.

"And this," he said, walking a little farther.

"Toothwort. The only others I've seen are trillium." She left the path and went poking through the understory until she came to the moss-covered boulders. He was right behind her. She knelt in front of a plant with three mottled green leaves. "They're called *tri*llium because everything's in threes. Before long these chutes will open into a three-leafed flower." The girl was quiet as if she was pondering whether to tell him something.

He lowered himself close enough to notice the skirt of her dress touching his leg and gently ran his fingers across the plant's leaves. "I hope I'm around to see it," he said, as if talking more to himself than to her.

"It's my favorite flower," she said. They studied the trillium without speaking. She turned to face him. "I just realized; I've never told anyone that before."

After an awkward silence, she spoke up. "That seems to be it for now. Dutchmen's breeches will be out in a few days, and after that, larkspur. When we move closer to summer, the glade flowers will bloom."

"Glade?"

"The rocky opening back there. It's called a glade. Did you see the cactus?"

"Cactus in Middle Tennessee?"

"Follow me."

They stood in unison, and she led him to the edge of the glade. "Well I'll be," he said. "Prickly pear."

"It blooms in late May or early June, a glossy yellow flower like it's covered in candle wax, one of my favorites."

The captain stared at the cactus for a few seconds. "I'll have to take your word for it. I don't know where I'll be when it blooms, but it won't be here. We didn't come south to loll around Murfreesboro."

After another period of silence, she walked past him, and he followed her back to the bluff. She stopped at the gazebo entrance.

"Here, let me move that," he said, stepping around her to pick up his valise. He'd set it where he suspected she always sat. A surprising wave of sadness washed over him as he thought about leaving.

"I didn't mean to run you off, Captain Lockridge."

"I do so like this place."

"You don't have to leave on my account."

I guess no one else is coming after all, he thought, and took a seat, not next to her, but catty-cornered so that a section of the seven-sided bench separated them.

"Tell me about Kenyon College," she said.

"It's in the middle part of Ohio."

"An Episcopal college, I believe."

"Started by Bishop Chase in the twenties."

"I imagine it was a stimulating experience."

He found himself brimming with enthusiasm telling her about a part of his life the war had pressed to the back of his mind, describing his courses, his teachers, his fellow students.

He was particularly animated relating his examination of the natural world in the marsh down by the Kokosing River.

"It's an experience I regret I'll never have," she said.

He noticed a sharp change in the tone of her voice. "I suppose you're right."

"Suppose? Do you know of any full-fledged college for someone of my sex?"

"I guess not." He looked away, and then back at her. "But you're clearly educated; surely you've had schooling."

"At the Nashville Female Academy, which you've probably never heard of."

"You forget that our army was quartered in Nashville before the battle."

"Well, it's in a sorry state now."

"That depends on one's perspective; it's being used as a hospital to treat our sick and wounded."

"What building isn't? Your army has taken over every public building."

"Miss Blaylock, let me remind you that your own church was first used as a hospital by the Rebel army." He was eager to change the subject. "About your education, do you perceive that it was deficient?"

"Yes and no." There was a heavy emphasis on reading and composition, as well as on Greek and Latin, she explained. They'd studied philosophy, mathematics, astronomy, chemistry, and of course botany. It was a rigorous education, particularly for girls, and she said, looking back, she liked that aspect of it.

When he asked what she meant by the "no" part of her answer, he noticed her back stiffen and a tightness in her neck.

"Dr. Elliott, the headmaster, didn't want us to be independent thinkers," she told him through tight lips. With an intensity he hadn't noticed before, she related that the headmaster had gone so far as to fire a respected teacher for suggesting that by becoming educated, the girls might someday lead independent lives. "And he said we should be protected from what he called 'strong-minded women' who would infect us with 'mannishness of mind and soul.' We were to be 'sweetly submissive,' to use his words. His primary objective was to train us to be wives and mothers."

The captain thought for a second before he responded. "I don't see the harm in training girls to be wives and mothers."

"I'm not saying there is." She went on to explain that now that the prospect for marriage had been snatched from her, she was considering alternatives. She didn't see why marrying the right man, or marrying at all, should be the only way a woman has to distinguish herself. She'd come around to thinking that independence was what she desired most in life. "There are times when I don't think I can be dependent on … I'll come right out and say it, Captain, dependent on any man."

"How can you say that the prospect of marrying has been taken from you? You're a young woman."

"There was a man I assumed I'd marry, but this cruel war has taken him from me."

So she did meet someone here. "I'm sorry."

"There is another aspect of this."

"Of what?"

"My changed attitude. The longer this vicious war drags on, there'll be fewer and fewer men. So you see, my resolve to live independently makes perfect sense."

"But not necessarily for all young women."

"That's why a few of them are keeping company with your men. They're desperate."

"Perhaps they're the lucky ones."

"If they marry and leave. But if they're courted by a man who never returns for them, their lives here will be ruined."

***

In Camp, M'boro, Tenn.
April 9, '63

My Dearest Miranda,

I have no war news since my last letter. We're still stuck in this place. Gen'l Bradley believes that now that spring has arrived, we could move out any day, but he doesn't know any more than the rest of us. We continue to hear rumors that Washington is getting after Old Rosey pretty hard about taking on Bragg again.

Spring is coming into full bloom down here, and today I broke the tedium by wandering into some woods. I bought a notebook to record aspects of nature, and today, my first day at it, I recorded four species of blooming flowers as well as blooming redbud trees and dogwood about to bloom. I even found a cactus that I'm told blooms in May or June.

I'm not sure if I told you about the gazebo atop a bluff above the river on the widow's farm. It's a quiet and peaceful spot, and I returned there today. I had intended to write this letter from there, but didn't get to. Maybe next time.

Ma's last letter said you're as beautiful as ever and you don't seem to be eaten up with worry like so many. I'm relieved to hear that. Right now, there is nothing to worry about other than sickness. We do have lots of men getting sick.

That's it for now. I miss you.

Your loving fiancé,
John

***

Four or five days had passed since Carrie had seen Captain Lockridge, and she had to admit that she wouldn't mind if he showed up again. She was getting to enjoy the company. So, sitting by herself at the gazebo, she was pleased when she heard him call her name from the edge of the woods.

"I was hoping to find you here," he said, walking to the entrance.

"I have something for you." Carrie pulled from the pocket of her dress a piece of paper and handed it to him.

He unfolded it. "A trillium. Where did you find this?"

"I drew it."

"You didn't tell me you're an artist." He studied the drawing. "It's quite good."

"Thank you," she responded, not the least bit ashamed of her pride.

He reached to return it to her.

"It's yours to keep," she said, trying unsuccessfully to repress a grateful smile.

"That's kind of you. I'll keep it with my important papers."

"With the letters from your fiancée?"

"How did you know I save her letters?"

"You seem like the type." She thought she saw him blush. "I'll bet you keep them in chronological order, too, maybe even tied together with a ribbon or some string?"

"You're quite perceptive, Miss Blaylock."

"What's she like?"

"Who?"

"Your fiancée."

"She's pretty."

"I'm sure she is, but surely you have more to say about her."

"Her name's Miranda Escobar, and as I said before, she's of Spanish ancestry."

"Is she fluent in Spanish?"

"Somewhat," he said with a chuckle. "She uses it when she doesn't want others to know what she's saying."

"Would that include you?"

"Sometimes. I've threatened to master the language to keep her from doing it."

He's such a smart man, Carrie thought. He shouldn't have any trouble mastering Spanish. I'm sure he's already versed in Latin. "And her family?" Carrie asked.

He explained that she's the youngest of four daughters, so much younger, it's like she's an only child. The captain chuckled again. "There are those who think she's spoiled."

"Not you, I hope."

"Not me."

"Your mother does, I'll bet."

The captain paused. "You *are* perceptive."

"I was raised in a family in which a brother took a wife."

"Some things are universal I suppose, North and South."

"Mothers are mothers," Carrie said, "though my mother thinks highly of her daughter-in-law. What are your wedding plans?"

"Not until the war ends. That was a condition of our engagement."

So the girl doesn't want to be widowed, Carrie thought. I can't blame her for that.

They sat quietly, listening to the ripple of the Stones River.

"It's taken quite an effort to get to this point."

"To what point?"

"Our engagement."

"Oh?"

He explained that her family is of the Roman faith, each of her sisters married someone of that faith, and that it took a while to get her father's consent. The captain gave a little laugh that seemed to Carrie to be forced. "He held out until I was in the thick of the fight, thinking that maybe I won't make it and she'll be free to marry a Catholic."

"That's terrible," Carrie said. "Surely you don't believe that."

"Just joking."

"Tell me, does she enjoy reading as much as you?"

"Not really. I mean she does read, but not like …" The captain didn't say anything for a few seconds.

"What were you going to say?"

"She doesn't like to read like you and I do."

They sat for a full minute taking in the reassuring sights and sounds of the dawning spring before she stood and walked to the woods. He followed her to the trillium. It was now in full bloom.

***

Rain mixed with chunks of wet snow falling from low-hanging clouds made it a good day for Carrie to stay indoors and take her rest with a book by the fire. But she hadn't seen the captain in a while and sensed that today he would come, bad weather or not. So she bundled up and trudged through the mud down the path to the bluff. Sure enough, he was there.

"Hello, Captain," she said, walking into the gazebo.

"Ah, Miss Blaylock, I was wondering if you'd venture out in this mess. I'm glad you did." He stood.

"It's nice to see you again."

She took her usual seat. He did the same.

"It's not much of a day for flowers," he said.

"No, and besides, I haven't seen any new ones blooming since you were here … when was it?"

"Let's see, I believe it was last Thursday. Today's Monday, so that would be four days ago." He paused for an instant. "For some reason, it seems longer." He paused again. "What did you bring?"

"Bring?"

"For us to read."

Carrie was embarrassed. "I walked out without a book. Let me run back. I've selected one we both should enjoy."

"Don't bother, unless you really want to. I take pleasure in our conversations, and there is something I need to discuss with you."

"Discuss with *me*?"

He shifted uncomfortably.

"If I crossed a line in our conversation last time, please forgive me."

She was unsure how to respond. "Thank you, but I have no idea what you're talking about."

"Telling you all about my fiancée."

"You didn't tell me much."

"I suppose not, though actually, there's not much more to tell. Anyway, I've been thinking that perhaps I was too personal."

A disquieting sensation came over Carrie that showed in her voice.

"I asked you, didn't I?"

"Yes, but—"

"You thought I was just asking to be nice? Let me assure you I wasn't just being nice."

"I guess you weren't. No, that didn't sound right. What I meant was …"

"There's nothing for you to apologize for," Carrie replied firmly.

"Thank you. I've been worried that I crossed a line."

"Again, didn't I ask you about, what's her name, Meredith?"

"Miranda."

"Yes, Miranda, Spanish. Didn't I ask you?"

"Yes, but—"

"Yes, but you don't think a woman can take the initiative in a conversation with a man."

"No, not at all. Well, perhaps I did."

"Perhaps I'm not like the other women you know. Perhaps I'm not like your sisters."

"My sisters?"

"You said the other day you'd be proud to have me as a sister."

"I meant that as a compliment."

"I took it that way."

"Can I be honest with you?"

"Haven't you been honest all along?"

"I didn't mean it like that."

"How did you mean it?"

"Miss Blaylock, no disrespect to my sisters, who I love dearly, but …"

"Your sisters?"

"You mentioned my sisters. I was about to say that I find you much more … how to put it … more engaging than either of them."

Carrie was struck by the awareness that something she didn't understand had gotten into her, so she forced a smile and changed the subject. "Are there many women teachers in Columbus, Ohio?"

"Teachers?"

"School teachers."

"The Romans have their nuns."

"I mean in secular schools."

"We have common schools supported by taxes. There are some women teachers, lots more now that the men are off to war. Then there are subscription schools owned by women. My sisters received a fine education at one. Why do you ask?"

"Since we've arrived at a level of familiarity, I don't mind telling you; I'm considering making that my career."

"There's certainly no higher calling than educating young minds. So you're definitely going to forgo marriage?"

"That's my plan, but who knows, maybe there's a man who'd accept having a wife with a career of her own."

"I can't think of any female teachers who are married. There are those who start teaching unmarried, but of course …"

"They're forced to quit when they marry."

"I wouldn't put it quite like that. It's just that … well …"

"A woman can't be in two places at once any more than a man, is that what you meant to say?"

"Not exactly, but you get the point."

"Well, let me tell you, Captain. I'm not going to waste my energy fretting over choosing between motherhood and a career when my chance of having a career now seems more likely than being a mother."

"Perhaps you sell yourself too short. You're still quite young, as I mentioned the other day."

"We've plowed this ground before."

"I suppose we have. It's just that …"

"Just what?"

"You seem to have so much to offer."

"I'm flattered you think so."

The captain paused. "You asked about my fiancée. Tell me about yours."

The question stunned Carrie. She most certainly didn't want to talk about it. But, she thought, I have no right to ask him prying questions and not let him do the same. "His name was Grantland Harvey, and we were not officially engaged. But everyone expected that when the time was right, we'd marry. He was my brother's closest friend growing up, and they'd become partners in law practice, though obviously that didn't last long. They were just getting started."

"Why didn't you marry him?"

"Father didn't believe it was suitable for an educated woman to marry before turning twenty-one. And he wanted me to further my education. I'd planned on returning to Philadelphia for a year or maybe two to attend one of the more selective female seminaries. But of course, the war killed that idea."

"Your father must have valued your intellect."

"I don't know if that's how I'd put it, but Father did encourage me to broaden myself." She gave a small laugh. "Travis, my brother, teased that I was Father's favorite."

"Were you?"

"Of course not. But …"

"But what?"

"Father did appreciate me in a way not many men would. It wasn't so obvious to me at the time."

"Did your father disapprove of Grantland for a husband?"

"On the contrary, he liked and respected him. Father said it was just a question of timing. But looking back on it, I have the feeling there was more to it, that he saw the potential for a life that didn't conform to the expectations for a Southern lady."

"You could have married after you father's death, after the war snuffed out your education plans."

"He was wise in so many ways, and I wanted to honor Father's wishes even after he was gone, so I decided to wait until I turned twenty-one. Father couldn't have predicted it, but not marrying Grantland probably worked out for the best."

"What do you mean by that?"

"I'd be a widow and probably a widow with a child. Many women in that predicament live in constant fear, even more than the rest of us."

"A second marriage is not out of the question."

"But, as we discussed, there are fewer and fewer eligible men every day."

"Your brother's widow, how do you see her making out?"

"Who knows? She's certainly not panicked like some girls."

"Panicked?"

"They're eaten up with fear and apprehension, particularly the ones with children. Why else do you think some of them are—"

"Letting our boys court them?"

"Yes."

They sat in silence.

"Do I seem like a lunatic?" asked Carrie, with a change in the tone of her voice.

"What kind of question is that?"

"My desire to live independently."

"You don't seem like a lunatic, Miss Blaylock."

The rain mixed with snow turned to solid snow while they sat engrossed in conversation under the protection of the gazebo roof. When it was time to go, they walked together through the slush to the glade, both commenting on how beautiful it was, the wet April snow clinging to the light green growth of spring.

"Like a clean white sheet covering it all up," she said, "the filth of war."

"Too bad it can't snow every day," he said with a laugh.

"Not a pleasant thought for men living in tents," she said, also laughing.

"I guess not. Good day, Miss Blaylock. I hope we're able to visit again."

"So do I, Captain." She turned and left the glade along the narrow path through the cedars.

***

Captain Lockridge had tethered his horse on the same tree he had on his other visits. Mounting, he recalled noticing that the girl always sat in the same spot and how she must derive comfort from the routine. I'm no different, he thought.

He spent his time riding back to camp in the falling wet snow thinking about being alone with her. She was so trusting of him, and she was clearly receptive to his visits; why else would she come out on such a day. But the last few times, she'd seemed … he couldn't put his finger on the right word. Her voice had an edge to it. I suppose it's too much to ask someone who's lost a brother and a fiancé—almost a fiancé—to always be sweet and kind to an enemy soldier.

The more he thought about it, the more he wondered if his friendship with the girl was ending. Do I want to be with her if she's going to … he couldn't come up with the right description. Perhaps I shouldn't go there anymore. But I do so love that place. And I enjoy the girl's company even if she does at times get testy. He tried to turn his mind to something else, but the girl lingered in his thoughts. Actually, he said to himself, I rather like her spunk. There's nothing wrong with a little backbone in a woman.

***

No horse within fifty miles of Murfreesboro was secure. General Rosecrans had declared that he wouldn't start the next campaign until he'd accumulated at least 70,000 horses and mules, and he had a long way to go to reach that number. And, too, he'd authorized the mounting of Colonel John T. Wilder's infantry brigade, and his men were scouring the countryside taking every horse they found. It didn't matter that so many women would be left with no way to plow and that they, along with the children, might face starvation. It was war. It was only a matter of time before the Blaylock farm would be deprived of its one remaining horse.

In the division of labor Amanda Blaylock decreed, Cassie was in charge of farming. After getting her opinion, Amanda decided that they should go ahead with their spring planting—even if it was wetter than it should be—while they still had a horse to pull the plow. So everyone on the place took to the fields. Sampson struggled with the plow behind the old draft horse, and the four females followed setting out corn, Irish potatoes, cabbage, and peas. They were in the field from sunup to sundown for three straight days.

***

Carrie wasn't used to that kind of work. Her back ached, and it was a relief to return to the gazebo to rest. Whether the captain would show up, she didn't know. She never did, but she hoped he would. She was getting to like him. So her heart pumped a little faster when she heard the rustling on the path behind her.

But it wasn't the captain.

Two other men in blue walked up beside the gazebo. One came to the entrance.

"What have we here, Artman?" he said.

"Don't bother the girl, Heflin," said the one standing away from the gazebo.

"I won't do anything with her she won't like," said the one at the entrance, turning his attention to Carrie. "You look lonely out here all by yourself."

"Stop it, Heflin." The other soldier walked closer to the entrance. "We're trying to find the ford to cross the river. How do we get there?"

"I don't know of any ford around here," Carrie said.

"Someone must have given us bad directions, because they said there's one up this way," said the man called Artman.

"If you go upstream you'll come to the Salem Pike, and you can cross there," said Carrie, relieved that the second man seemed intent on leaving.

"We can't cross on no public road," said Heflin, the scary one.

"Well that's the best I can do," said Carrie, hoping they would leave.

"Sorry to have troubled you. Let's go."

"Not so fast," Heflin said. "We might be able to give this lonely looking girl some company for a few minutes."

"Leave the girl alone, Heflin."

"What about it, little lady, wouldn't you like to cuddle with a couple of strong men? We can show you some things I'll bet you've never seen."

The man took a step inside the gazebo, and when he did, Carrie bolted for the entrance.

"Hold it, girl," he said, clutching her arms. "Let's you and me snuggle a little." He forced her back onto the seat and stood over her.

Carrie couldn't tell what it was or where it was, but there was an explosion.

"Get your hands in the air, both of you."

She was uncertain what she was hearing. "Carrie, come here!"

She recognized the captain's voice and dashed out of the gazebo to him.

"Get behind me."

She did as he said.

"Who are you bastards and what are you doing here? What's your regiment?" Using both hands, he aimed his revolver at the soldier in the gazebo.

"I don't figure that's none of your business," the man said.

"I'll tell you who we are," the other man, Artman, said. "We're two men who signed on to fight for the Union, and we're not staying around to fight for the niggers."

"That's right, Captain," Heflin said. "We didn't sign on to get ourselves killed for niggers. And we sure as hell ain't going to fight alongside 'em. We got paid today, and we're going to skedaddle."

"I should arrest both of you."

"You'll have a rough time of it, taking on two men. One of the three of us is likely to get killed, and it may be you."

No one spoke for a few seconds. The captain kept his revolver on the man doing the talking.

"But we'll make a deal with you. You can have this little secesh girl first. We don't mind going second and third do we, Artman? Just like with the whores in Nashville."

"You shut your mouth, Heflin," said the other man, looking at the captain. "I didn't mean the girl no harm, Captain. I was just asking her for directions, that's all."

"What about it, Captain," Heflin said. "She's a pretty little thing. Soft sandy hair, bright blue eyes, a few freckles on her rosy cheeks. Why just looking at her, I'd say you'll be the first man to have her. Wouldn't that be nice?"

The captain walked closer to Heflin, keeping his revolver aimed at him. He glanced at the other man and looked back to the gazebo entrance. "What did you say?"

"She don't look like she's had any experience with men, and you may be the first one to get her, a nice virgin for you. What about it?"

There was another explosion, and it took Carrie a second to comprehend what had happened. She saw a red spot appear on the man's face and his hat fly as he fell outside the gazebo.

"Don't shoot me, Captain! Tell him, miss, I didn't mean you no harm! Go ahead, miss, tell him!"

"Carrie, leave."

"You shot him!" she yelled.

"Goddamnit, Carrie, get the hell out of here! Now!"

She turned and ran toward the glade as fast as she could, feeling pushed by what she'd just witnessed. Crossing the rise in the hardwoods, she tripped over her long skirt and fell forward. "Oh," she cried at the pain in her wrists breaking the fall. She scrambled to her feet and hurried into the glade where she stopped. She needed to catch her breath and try to make sense of what she'd seen.

Carrie was suddenly seized by an odd awareness: I've touched the dying and the dead, but until now in this war, I haven't seen anyone get killed. Maybe he's not dead. No, he's dead, she said to herself, the image of his flying skull and brains fresh in her mind. She stood trembling trying to figure out what to do when she heard another shot.

"Oh my God," she said out loud, "he's killed the other one." She went on, walking as fast as she could through the cedars until she reached the edge of the thicket by the house. Prompted by a fear that the captain might show up there, she made for the barn and ducked into one of the clean back stalls.

Slumped to the ground, she pulled her knees to her chest and rocked back and forth trying to compose herself. Looking at her stinging hands, she saw a few spots of blood where the rocks had broken her skin in the fall. As she wiped them on the clean straw, she heard the captain coming into the barn. The pitchfork. She could protect herself with it. She stood and reached for it.

"Miss Carrie?"

Carrie slumped back to the ground as Cassie opened the stall door.

"Oh, Cassie," she said in a quivering voice, looking up at the woman standing over her. "He killed them, he killed them both."

"Who got killed? Who did the killing?"

"Didn't you hear the shots?"

"Child, we're always hearing shots around here these days. I didn't think nothing of it."

"It was the captain."

"Someone done shot the captain?"

"No, no, he shot them, two of them. He didn't have to … he didn't have to shoot them. He even shot the one who … " As she tried to explain, she started sobbing and shaking.

Cassie eased down beside her and pulled her close.

"Just let it all out child, let it all out, whatever it is."

When Carrie ceased heaving, she pushed herself away. "It's all my fault."

"I'm not following you."

"If it hadn't been for me, none of this would have happened. It's all because of me. Two men are dead. Oh, Cassie, I feel so ashamed."

"What is it, Miss Carrie, what are you trying to tell me?"

"Two deserters came upon me at the bluff. One of them said he was going to … it's too horrible to say. The captain shot him. And he shot the other one. I caused it all."

"Now you look a' here, Miss Carrie, if you was going to tell me what I think, it ain't your fault. Do you hear me? It ain't your fault. You didn't cause nothing."

"But if I hadn't been …"

"I don't want to hear it."

"But they …"

"You hush girl. I'll tell it to you straight out: ain't no man has a right to take from a woman what they was going to take from you without her say-so. You hear? No man. Them men got just what was coming to 'em."

"He didn't have to shoot them. He could have just arrested them." She paused for a few seconds. "Cassie, it makes me afraid of him, afraid to be around him."

"Afraid of the captain? Sounds to me like you got it backward. He saved you."

"But did he have to shoot them both? I mean, the second one, he didn't … I can't say it. It's too awful."

"Miss Carrie, you remember that boy from Kentucky who they caught running off from the Rebel army when they was here?"

"Sure."

"And what did old Bragg do?"

"Had him shot."

"That poor boy was just trying to get home to see after his widowed mama. They shoot deserters. And what they said they was going to do to you, why Old Rosecrans himself would string 'em up from the nearest tree if he found out about it. Shootin' be too good for 'em. The captain, he just saved the army the trouble. Them men was probably no 'count to begin with."

"I don't know."

"Well I do. Let me tell you something, Miss Carrie. I've seen a few things in my life. You'll just have to trust me. They deserved to be shot. That's a fact."

"I'd better go tell Mother." Carrie stood and dusted off her dress.

"Your mama ain't back from town just yet. Now you go up to your room and get some rest. Ain't nobody going to bother you in the house, least not while I'm around. You and Miss Amanda can sort it all out when she gets back."

When they reached the barn door, Cassie stopped and took Carrie by the arm. "Promise me, Miss Carrie, there won't be no more thinking it's you fault. And there won't be any more thinking 'bout being afraid of the captain. Will you promise me that?"

"I'll try."

Carrie gave the black woman a hug and walked to the house.

***

She awoke to a soft knock on the door to her room with no idea how long she'd been asleep.

"May I come in?" It was her mother.

"Yes."

Amanda sat on the bed. "I'm sorry about what happened."

"Who told you?"

"Cassie. And the captain."

"The captain?" A jolt of fear charged through Carrie. "He's here?"

"He was."

"Oh, Mother, I'm so ashamed."

"Carrie, my dear, you have nothing to be ashamed of."

"That's what Cassie said."

"You must accept that, and you must try to put this behind you. It'll help when you talk to him."

"Talk to him? It's too embarrassing, the things that man said, right in front of him. I don't want to ever see him again."

"You two should have a talk. It'll help you get beyond it."

"I hope he doesn't come back."

"He will."

***

The pounding in John's head only got worse as he made his morning rounds through the regiments. Sleep had eluded him. Every time he drifted off he saw the image of the deserter with half his head blown away and of the other with a bloodstained bullet hole in his chest. He'd witnessed hundreds of men getting blown to bits in the battle, but for some reason, these killings stayed with him.

Rolling around on his cot, he'd spent much of night arguing with himself.

I'm a noble soldier protecting a helpless woman.

I'm a cold-blooded murderer.

The deserter was right; it would have been impossible to take them in. They'd be headed for a firing squad, so they had nothing to lose.

If I'm the noble soldier, then why did I go to so much trouble to remove any trace of them?

I should report it.

That would only complicate my life. Nothing good would come of it.

They got what was coming to them.

Returning to headquarters after his rounds, the captain handed his horse to an orderly and nervously stepped inside the big tent. He'd decided upon a course of action that he hoped would relieve his anxiety.

"What's going on here?" he asked entering the tent. Most of the brigade staff officers were standing around the table with an upside down hat resting on it.

"A game of chance," General Bradley said. "We've each written on a scrap of paper what we think our next campaign will be. And we've each put in fifty cents. I'll keep the money, and whoever wins will get it at the end of the campaign. Want in, Lockridge?"

The Confederate Army of Tennessee was twenty miles to the south protected by the range of rugged hills separating the watersheds of the Cumberland and Tennessee Rivers. The hills gave out around Shelbyville on the west of the Rebels' front. Their lifeline south was the railroad to Chattanooga. Taking the situation into account, the captain asked what options had been selected.

His friend Marshall answered. The first was that Rosecrans would take the path of least resistance, bypass the hills, and head straight south to hit the west end of the Rebel line at Shelbyville. The second option was that the army would march directly east across the Cumberland Plateau, descend into the Tennessee Valley, and take Chattanooga from the north. Bragg would have to retreat to protect the railroad to Atlanta. The third was similar to the second, only once in the valley, the Federals would go in the opposite direction, up to Knoxville and meet up with Burnside's army coming south out of Kentucky. The fourth option was that half the army would stay put at Murfreesboro to keep Bragg occupied while the other half would go to Mississippi to help Grant take Vicksburg. The fifth option was that President Lincoln would finally get fed up with Rosecrans's inaction, and remove him from command.

"All right, I'll join in," John said.

"What's your option, number six?"

"Rosecrans will send us through the hills right down the Manchester Turnpike on the east end of the Rebel line to try to get between the Johnnies and Chattanooga. Cut off from his line of supply and retreat, Bragg will have no choice but to turn around and fight."

"Write it down, initial it, and put it in the hat with your coin," said General Bradley. A lull in the conversation followed.

"General, can I have a word with you?" asked John, trying to hide his nervousness.

"What is it, Lockridge?"

"Privately, if you don't mind, sir."

He and the young general stepped outside the headquarters tent.

"You recall the assignment you gave me back in the winter to investigate the theft of pigs from a widow woman and my report to you about it?"

"Certainly. Just the other day I was wondering about the widow's daughter, the one I encountered on the cars. How is the girl?"

"That's what I want to discuss with you. I've returned to the widow's some and become acquainted with the family."

"I didn't think you've been absenting yourself from headquarters to find a card game."

"No, sir."

"I've tolerated it as long as it doesn't interfere with your duties."

"Yes, sir. I bring this to your attention because the family and the girl you met have been molested again by soldiers."

"I detest that behavior, Lockridge," said the brigadier, "but it's becoming more common. I suspect you've brought this up for some reason other than your concern for discipline in the Union army."

"Yes, sir."

"What is it?"

"Many staff officers are billeting in private homes, and I thought that perhaps if I did, at the widow's, for the short period we're still here, it would offer some measure of protection for her and the family."

General Bradley thought for a few seconds. "It meets with my approval for one of my men to do a good deed for a defenseless widow and her daughters. She has two, I believe, the one I met and another one."

"Yes, sir, a younger girl."

"When did you have in mind?"

"As soon as I can get my things together."

"I don't see why you should wait."

"Thank you, sir."

As John took a few steps in the direction of his hovel, he turned when he heard the general call his name.

"Lockridge?"

"Yes, sir."

"Don't get mixed up in anything you'll regret."

"Don't worry, sir."

***

Sitting alone on the porch later that day struggling to concentrate on a book, Carrie looked up to the sound of a rider approaching and saw John emerging from the orchard. Her back stiffened as she pondered how she'd react to him.

"Hello," he said after securing his horse and taking a seat in a rocker.

"Hello," she said. As they sat without speaking, Carrie was relieved that she didn't feel the embarrassment she'd anticipated. And she was surprised that she didn't find their extended silence uncomfortable.

He spoke first. "Carrie, I'm sorry for what happened out there yesterday."

It was at least a half a minute before she spoke. "It's not your fault either." She paused again. "You saved me, John, you saved me from … they might have killed me."

"Those two men will never bother anyone again."

Carrie thought again about that second shot. "So you did shoot the other one?"

"It's over, Carrie. It's not something we need to discuss further. I have something more important to talk about."

"What?"

"Us."

"Us?"

"Me and your family. I'm going to start billeting in your house."

"Where? When?

"In your father's study. I'll start tonight."

"How can you do that? You have duties."

"Officers are living all over in people's houses. I'm just one more. I've already cleared it with General Bradley."

"Does he remember me?"

"Of course he remembers you." John was quiet for a second. "I can't be here every night. I've explained that to your mother. I'll try to come up with some way to scare people away when I'm not here. And I don't know how long it will last. We could move out any day."

"I suppose I should be grateful."

"You don't sound like you are."

"I'm sorry, John. It's just that it all seems so strange all of a sudden. But then, everything's been strange for a long time."

"This war's hard on everyone."

"I am grateful, really I am. It'll just take some getting used to, that's all. But it's not like it's something new, having a man around."

"Remember, I'm the same age as your brother."

***

Carrie fidgeted in the parlor straightening curtains that didn't need straightening and rearranging books that didn't need rearranging. Why am I so embarrassed, she asked herself. It's not like I've never seen a bare-chested man. I do have a brother, or did. She recalled, too, at age thirteen or fourteen when she and some friends snuck to the riverbank to spy on Travis and his friends bathing in the twilight. They'd seen a lot more than bare chests. And of course, there was no time for modesty tending the wounded after the battle.

She'd awakened as usual at the first rooster crow, washed her face with the pitcher of water she'd set out the night before, exchanged her nightgown for a dress, and stepped quickly down the stairs and out to the kitchen. Her face went crimson when she walked in on John standing in front of the stove, naked above the waist.

"Good morning," he said.

"Uh, good morning."

"It looks like a fine spring day. I slept like a baby."

His blue uniform pants were tucked into his boots, and his suspenders dangled beside his thighs. He turned to continue shaving in front of the little mirror he'd propped up on the shelf. "I'll be done in a minute."

She stayed in the parlor until she heard him close the door to the study, the room her mother had given him to sleep in. Carrie returned to the kitchen. I don't know what my reaction was all about, she thought, but one thing's for certain; life around here will be different, for a little while at least.

She fetched the milk pail and let herself out the kitchen door.

***

The next morning she didn't see John until she tramped through the crisp air back to the kitchen lugging the pail of milk. He opened the door for her.

"Thank you," she said. "I'll have your breakfast in a minute."

She excused herself and went outside and into the cellar. It was cool, like in a cave. She picked up three of the eggs that Cassie had collected the day before and cut off several slices of a ham. Back in the kitchen, John sat at the table while she busied herself preparing the meal.

She broke the eggs over a big beige ceramic mixing bowl and beat them to a frothy yellow. She scooped cornmeal from a crock and stirred it into the eggs. When the lumps dissolved, she dipped a cup into the milk bucket and added some to the cornmeal mix a little at a time, stirring until she got the right consistency. She then poured some of the mix onto the griddle.

"I warned you yesterday that wheat flour is in short supply around here," said Carrie over her shoulder. "We haven't had any for … let's see, after I got back from Nashville, except for what you brought at Easter, so corn cakes are all I can offer."

"They were tasty yesterday, and I'm sure they will be today. And your ham, it's outstanding."

This morning, the second day of having a boarder, Carrie didn't feel so nervous, which was a relief. And she wasn't afraid of John like she thought she might be after witnessing him shoot the deserters. "It's nice of you to start the fire and get the water, but it's not necessary," she said.

"It's the least I can do."

She turned to face him. "You do know, John, from our standpoint, you're doing quite a bit just staying here."

"I hope so, but I can't guarantee it will fully protect you."

"It makes us feel better just the same." She looked him squarely in the eyes. "That's half the battle isn't it?"

"Battle?"

"To feel secure even if it's an illusion." Carrie turned back to the stove. "I hope I'm not wearing you out with my fears."

"Not at all." He paused. "I'm flattered you feel comfortable enough around me to share your feelings."

"I feel the same. By the way, I forgot to tell you yesterday. One of the many items that have disappeared from Southern kitchens is coffee, so I can't offer you any."

"Oh, that reminds me." The captain left and returned with a tin. "Coffee. I bought some yesterday."

"Well, now I don't feel so bad," Carrie said with a smile. "I'll have it ready for you in an instant."

"Ready for *us*, I bought the coffee for all of us, not just for myself."

"Now that's just wonderful, John. Be sure Mother pays you."

"I won't need any reimbursement for a while."

Carrie's heart raced, recalling that the deserters said they'd just been paid, but her rise of fear fell quickly.

"What's that I smell?" asked Amanda Blaylock, emerging from the passageway into the kitchen.

"Good morning, ma'am," said the captain, rising from the table.

"That smells like coffee."

"It is, Mother. The captain brought us coffee."

"Well, I declare," Amanda exclaimed. "I can't recall the last time I had real coffee."

***

The following morning, Carrie awoke to the aroma of coffee, and walking into the kitchen, she found John at the table.

"My, what wonderful service." He rose to greet her, and she couldn't contain her smile. "If someone had told me I'd be coming into our kitchen and there'd be a pot of coffee on the stove, I'd have told them they'd lost their mind."

"It's the least I can do. You folks are awfully good to me."

Carrie tied on her apron and took the milk pail from its peg. Opening the door, she turned back to the sound of his voice.

"Mind if I come along?"

She detected a hint of playfulness. They stood face to face for a few seconds in awkward silence.

"Or I'll wait here, if you like," he said.

"No, come on with me."

***

Carrie was glad it was Wednesday, her day to meet with her friends to read. She liked having John around, of that she was sure, but she was agitated by something, unable to understand what, and was hopeful Martha could help her sort it out.

"I don't know what it is," she said to her sister-in-law before the others arrived, "but when he asked if he could go to the barn with me, I felt … I don't know, rattled?"

They sat quietly for a moment before Martha spoke. "It seems different to me."

"What do you mean?"

"It's one thing to be with this unfamiliar man in broad daylight, but in a barn is something else."

"But we've been alone at the bluff just the two of us, and that didn't feel … I don't know how to put it, threatening?"

"A dimly lit barn shut off from the rest of the world—it seems different to me. I mean, think of all the stories we've heard about what goes on in barns," said Martha, showing a mischievous grin.

Carrie blushed, wondering if Martha knew about Christmas night and her time alone with the Louisiana lieutenant. "The captain's a gentleman in every way. I can't think of any cause to feel afraid."

Martha looked Carrie in the eye for a few seconds before she spoke. "Maybe it's not him you're afraid of."

***

The next morning was just like the last, only when John stood as Carrie walked into the kitchen, she greeted him differently. "John, I appreciate your courtesy, but it isn't necessary for you to rise when I enter the room." She paused. "You wouldn't do that for your sisters."

"Sisters?"

"You said a while back that you'd be proud to have me as a sister. When you lived in the same house with them, I'm sure you didn't react as you would to some other lady."

"Does it bother you?"

"Oh no, I rather like it, but I don't want you to feel burdened by having to mind your manners in these close quarters."

"I don't feel burdened, and if it's just the same to you, I'll continue to extend the same courtesy that I would to any lady."

***

John arrived as usual at brigade headquarters, saluted the general, and spoke to First Lieutenant Marshall. He was often full of questions about the widow, her daughters, and how it was going, but this morning, Marshall kept quiet. There was a stranger in the tent.

"Lockridge, this is Captain Goodman from the provost marshal's guard," General Bradley said.

John shook the man's hand.

"He has some questions for you."

"About what, sir?"

"I'll let him explain."

John turned to Captain Goodman.

"You've probably heard about the bodies of two soldiers washing up at Fortress Rosecrans."

"I'm aware of it," John said.

"I'm investigating it."

"Men are dropping dead like flies around here. Why is this of any consequence?"

"Because they'd been shot."

"It's war."

"There is a chance they were robbed. They'd just been paid, and if there was any chance they were killed for their money, it has to be investigated. There was no money on their bodies."

"Why not just check with their regiments."

"Whoever took their money also removed anything that might make their bodies easy to identify. Another reason we think they may have been robbed."

"Why does this involve me?" John was starting to feel tightness in his chest.

"It's likely that the killing took place along the river between the Franklin and Salem Pikes. Checking around, I've discovered that you're boarding at a farm there. You might have heard something."

"Like what?"

Captain Goodman related that the surgeon who examined their bodies determined that at least one of them, the one shot in the chest, had been killed by a revolver. "The other's head was too messed up to tell what hit him. Officers carry revolvers. I know about the girl who I issued a pass to back in February. Who else lives there?"

"Her mother, another daughter, a Negro woman, and her son."

"How old?"

"Who?"

"The boy."

"Seventeen or so."

"Maybe he got his hands on your revolver."

"I have it on me at all times. I sleep with it under my pillow."

"Some of these coloreds are pretty resourceful."

"Goodman, I'm sure no one but me has touched my revolver."

"I'd like to look at it just the same."

John felt blood rush to his face. In all the commotion and his strain afterwards, he'd neglected to replace the three rounds he'd fired at the bluff. He unfastened his holster and handed the man his weapon.

"Three rounds are missing," Goodman said.

"I trust that confirms this revolver wasn't used to shoot them."

"Why?"

"There would be only two rounds missing."

"But we don't know how many rounds the man took in the face."

"I suspect they were deserters who got what was coming to them."

"What makes you say so?"

"Because if they'd been shot anywhere near where they were supposed to be, someone would have witnessed it."

Captain Goodman looked at John with a slight grin. "You're a lawyer too, aren't you Lockridge?"

"I am."

"Do you think any of the women might know something?"

"There is nothing for them to know."

"Perhaps they heard something."

"I can't imagine what it would be."

"Still, it might be wise for me to interview them. You tell them I'll be coming by, will you?"

***

Carrie was pleasantly surprised to find a letter from her cousin Hugo LaBruce waiting for her the next time she stopped at the post office. She'd written him sometime ago asking him to make inquiries around Philadelphia. When time passed and she didn't hear back from him, she figured her letter had never made it to him, or if it had, his reply didn't make it to her.

He'd followed up on her request and asked around at several girls' schools about whether they'd consider employing as a teacher someone like her with no experience. Three had said yes, and he enclosed their names and addresses on a separate page.

***

The wedding of Olivia Hardison and Elton Stephenson took place under a cloudy, late April sky at his home next to the church he pastored. It was to be a small affair in the parlor, but a huge crowd showed up. Major Wiles, the provost marshal, was in a generous mood, and for this one day he relaxed the onerous restrictions that kept civilians from going in and out of the Federal lines. The last social event in Murfreesboro of this magnitude was Mattie Ready's wedding.

"Let's just move it outside," said Elton, taking Olivia by the hand and leading her into the crowd filling his lawn. A friend of his, a pastor from Bowling Green, had obtained a pass to travel to Murfreesboro to officiate.

It had been only a few weeks since Olivia had first confided in Carrie about Elton's proposal, and standing among the well-wishers, Carrie found the term "whirlwind courtship" popping into her mind. Back during the first months of the war when the Confederates were around, there was no end to the talk of girls marrying soldiers they'd known only briefly. Time will tell, everyone agreed, whether these marriages would survive. Many already hadn't, for every week another young woman was seen shrouded in black.

Carrie was pleased she'd been able to help Olivia sort out her thoughts and emotions in their several conversations. Yes, it might be better if he were closer to your age; yes, it might be better if he hadn't been married before; yes, it might be better if he didn't have two boys you'll have to raise; and yes, it might be better if you had a longer courtship. But these are unprecedented times, they both agreed. The old customs don't work anymore.

She's made the right choice, Carrie thought, as she listened to their vows.

***

On their way to the wedding, Amanda shared with her daughters that whenever she attended one, she recalled her own wedding. It struck Carrie as odd and maybe even morbid, but she found herself thinking about her wedding, the one that never happened. Theirs had been anything but a whirlwind courtship.

Grantland had always been around. Carrie hadn't given a moment's thought to any romantic interest in him or anyone else until her final year at the academy, the year she turned eighteen. She'd needed an escort to the spring formal, and her mother suggested Grantland. Carrie hesitated. She knew he'd go along with it; he was her brother's closest friend. But it'll seem like charity, she'd thought; he has no interest in me. She was wrong. Grantland confessed that weekend he'd always had something in mind for them.

Carrie was taken aback at first, but as the spring wore on and her graduation became imminent, she came to appreciate that a boy was actually interested in her; and not just any boy, but one who knew just about everything about her. They saw each other regularly that summer, and whenever Grantland took a break from his legal studies, he headed for the Blaylocks' farm. Then one evening in September as the weather was starting to cool, they slipped away to the gazebo. There in the twilight, Carrie did what he'd been after her to do ever since she came home from school in June. She kissed him.

***

It had been a while since Carrie had awakened in the middle of the night, but she was startled into alertness by images of an incident at the wedding. Following the vows, she was chatting with Olivia's cousin, Morton Walling, when a sudden commotion distracted them. One of Elton's boys, the oldest, had fallen out of a tree. Olivia darted from her new husband's side and pressed through the crowd to where the boy lay. Dr. Harvey, Grantland's father, was standing over him. "He's not hurt, just has the wind knocked out of him."

Olivia scooped up the boy, and when she did, he wrapped his arms around her neck and buried his head on her shoulder. When Elton reached them in a few seconds, Olivia informed him what the doctor had said and attempted to hand the boy to his father. But the boy wouldn't budge. He clung to Olivia while she stroked the back of his head: "You're going to be fine. You're just scared, that's all."

This incident replayed itself every time she started to fall asleep. There were so many nights when dreams of horrid experiences disturbed her, but why this, why something so warm, so tender? She lit the candle and opened her Bible to Luke.

> *And Mary said, Behold the handmaid of the Lord; be it unto me according to thy word. And the angel departed from her.*

CHAPTER FIVE

May 1863

The passing days slid into a routine for John Lockridge. He was usually the first to rise at the Blaylocks', and by the time Carrie came down to the kitchen, he'd drawn water from the well and had a fire crackling in the stove. He stood by her in the barn as she milked, and then he toted the full pail to the kitchen for her. He sipped his coffee at the table while she fixed breakfast, and they chatted as if they'd known each other their whole lives.

Sarah seemed to go out of her way to seek him out, which always cheered him. She was a lively and witty girl. And it didn't hurt that she was so pleasing to look at.

Amanda Blaylock treated John more like a son than a temporary border, and that comforted him, but he'd deny it if pressed. He continued his regular trips to the sutlers' wagons to buy food with the greenbacks from her hidden stash, and with his own money he made it a point to keep Carrie supplied with paper and pencils for her drawing.

Evenings usually found the two of them on the porch, reading aloud or engrossed in conversation. Other times they sat quietly listening for the whip-or-wills and hoot owls. Amanda often joined them. On other nights John and Carrie took advantage of the lengthening days to stroll out to the bluff where they sometimes sat without speaking while he watched her draw.

John wondered whether they'd run out of things to talk about, but they never did. He felt a burst of enthusiasm telling her about being in the crowd cheering President-elect Lincoln when he stopped in Columbus on his way to Washington. Something about the man's countenance had stayed with him, rendering him eager to volunteer when the new president called for troops to put down the rebellion.

"I can still see him," John said, "sometimes as clearly as he's standing next to me."

***

Ever since her mother had told John with some emotion that Carrie didn't go to town with them on Sundays anymore, he'd been curious about it, but Carrie always avoided it when he asked. This time, as they sat alone on the porch, she responded differently.

"All right, I'll tell you. I feel guilty about it, but it's Grantland's mother." Carrie had nothing against her, she explained. In fact, she was quite fond of her. But whenever they were together, Mrs. Harvey insisted on treating Carrie like she was her daughter-in-law. The woman would question Carrie about details of her life and offer unsolicited suggestions on all manner of topics, such as what dresses or hats she looked best in. Or Carrie's habit of letting her hair fall down in the back from a bow, which definitely didn't conform to the current fashion. "I sympathize with her, I really do, but I feel … what's the right word? Smothered? So I just avoid it. On Easter, at the church, I knew there'd be a big crowd, and I wouldn't be stuck with her. And, of course, I looked the way she thought I should that day." Carrie hesitated. "Do I sound terrible?"

"No, I understand completely."

They sat looking out over the orchard, taking in the sound of the chirping crickets before Carrie spoke.

"Since we're sharing deep secrets, I'll ask you about one." She reminded him of when they were first getting to know each other, and he said he suspected Miranda's father had consented to the marriage only because he thought John wouldn't make it home and she'd be free to marry a Catholic. "And you said you really didn't believe that?"

"I recall the conversation."

She looked him in the eye. "That's not completely true, is it? I mean, you at least suspected it, didn't you?"

John took a deep breath. "You're quite perceptive, Carrie."

They were quiet again before he brought up another subject she'd avoided. "You said your father opposed secession, but what about you?"

Carrie took her time answering. "I deferred to whatever opinion Father expressed."

"But you describe yourself as wanting to be independent, of not living subordinate to a man."

"I mean a husband, not my father. And besides, 1861 seems like a lifetime ago. The notion of having an opinion different from Father's never entered my mind then."

"Your father had passed by the time war broke out. Did that change your thinking?"

"Somewhat," Carrie said. She hadn't displayed the ebullience others had, but she went along with the prevailing sentiment. She helped sew flags and uniforms and delivered food to soldiers when they were around. She was part of the cheering throng when Travis, Grantland, and the other men marched off to the sound of martial music. But her mother's attitude served as a restraint. Amanda Blaylock saw her husband as a war casualty, convinced that strife in the community over secession killed him.

"Would your attitude have been different if your father hadn't passed?"

"I've wondered about that, quite a bit actually." Carrie explained that most folks in Middle Tennessee were like her father, against secession when it first came up and Tennessee voted it down. But after Lincoln's call for troops to go to war against the Deep South states, sentiment shifted dramatically. The congregation became solidly pro-secession. If her father had lived to express his opposition to Tennessee following the cotton states out of the Union, he'd surely have been forced to resign and possibly even leave town.

Travis would have joined the Confederates regardless, she said, and she couldn't see her mother leaving, with him in the army. "We might have ended up like the Forbeses' friends in Nashville, the mother staying and the father and daughters moving up North." Carrie related that she'd heard about the headmaster of a school up near Sparta with one son in the Confederate army and the other with the Federals. How tormented the man must be; how tormented the boys' sisters must be. On the other hand, if her father had joined the rush toward leaving the Union after Fort Sumter, he'd have violated his conscience.

They sat quietly for a moment before she spoke again. "It's a pretty grim time, isn't it?"

John thought carefully. "This may not be much of a consolation given your losses, but it's only through this war that we've become acquainted."

"I do treasure our friendship, John. Having a man as such a good friend is a new experience."

"Same here. I mean, having a woman for such a good friend."

"We wouldn't be permitted this luxury under the crusty old rules." In Southern society, respectable unmarried ladies weren't supposed to be alone with men outside courtship, and being alone even in courtship was frowned on in some circles. An innocent deviation from the dictates of propriety could ruin a girl's reputation. "Imagine that," Carrie laughed, "the dutiful, straight-laced, bookish—and some would say boring—Carrie Blaylock talked about as disreputable."

"I hadn't thought of it that way."

"This war is changing everything, John. So many of the old social rules are fading. Just look at my hands." She held them out, palms down. "It's essential for a Southern lady to have delicate hands. Mine are skinned up and raw from kitchen work."

"I don't see anything wrong with your hands." He gently took them in his.

***

John's tender gesture was still with Carrie a few days later as she hunched on all fours scrubbing the kitchen floor.

"You have a visitor."

Carrie rose to her knees at the sound of her mother's voice. "Who?"

"Elton Stephenson."

"Elton? What a surprise." She hadn't seen him since the wedding.

"He's on the front porch. I'll bring you something to drink."

Carrie stood, wiped her hands on her apron, hung it up, and made her way to him.

"It's nice to see you, Elton."

"It's nice to see you, Carrie."

"Have a seat," she said, directing him to one of the rockers. "How are the boys?" She took the chair facing him.

"Their lives have gotten better in the past few weeks."

"Olivia's a wonderful person, and I'm sure she's a loving and caring mother."

"You know, it's like she's always been their mother. Teddy, the youngest, you should've seen the look on his face the other day when she took a switch to his bare legs. I don't think it had dawned on him that she was going to be his mother in all respects. But he loves her even more, I think. Children are like that, you know? Deep in their hearts they know we discipline them because we love them."

"I've never had much occasion to give that any thought," she said.

"There's something else I'd like to discuss with you." When the schools had shut down, everyone expected it to be temporary. The war would be over in months. Now there wasn't any end in sight. "We can't stand by watching our children grow up uneducated," he said. He'd been talking to some other pastors about opening a school.

"A school sounds like a good idea. Where would it be?"

"We don't know. For now, it's more important that we find someone to run the school, and that's what I want to discuss with you."

"Me run a school?"

"Not exactly. You've met Olivia's cousin, Morton Walling. He's an experienced headmaster. He would be in charge. What we have in mind for you is teaching. Olivia told me of your ambition. Does that interest you?"

"Yes, but I figured I'd have to move somewhere else, up North even."

"I don't know how we'll finance it, which is a polite way of saying we won't be able to pay you at first. But we'll work on that later. I just want to confirm that you're interested."

"I am, most certainly."

***

Carrie stood before her full-length mirror pleased with what she saw. She'd selected her light-weight, sky-blue dress and a white lace collar and wore them with her favorite riding hat. She'd worn her dressy high-top shoes only once since the Nashville trip, on Easter, and she laced them before heading down the stairs. She seldom attracted attention in her usual get-up of a dreary homespun dress, big sunbonnet, and the Wellington boots her brother had outgrown. But being out in public dressed up, at least some of the horde of soldiers crammed around Murfreesboro would give her a second look. I don't have any choice, she thought; this may turn out to be one of the most momentous days of my life.

***

The handsome man with a missing right arm rose to greet Carrie as Olivia showed her into the sitting room of the house she now shared with Elton Stephenson.

"You remember my cousin, Morton Walling?"

"Yes, we visited at your wedding. It's a pleasure to see you again, Mr. Walling." She extended her gloved hand.

"The pleasure is mine, Miss Blaylock."

Carrie sensed by the way he turned his left hand that he wasn't yet comfortable using it. I wonder if he ever will be, she thought.

He was a tall man with brown hair receding about a quarter of the way back, exposing a high forehead. She spotted some gray on his temples. His only facial hair was a mustache that was a tad on the ragged side.

"I'll be back in a minute with something to drink," said Olivia, leaving the two of them alone.

They stood facing each other for a few seconds before he spoke. "Shall we have a seat, Miss Blaylock?"

"Yes, let's do, Mr. Walling."

Glancing around the room, Carrie noticed curtains and chair covers that hadn't been there on the day of the wedding. There were flowers, too, in a vase on the table. She felt a warm glow from these feminine touches.

"I understand from Elton that you're interested in joining us starting a school."

"Yes, I am, Mr. Walling. It's something I've had on my mind for a while, teaching that is. I've decided on it as a career. In thinking about it after Elton mentioned it, I concluded that this might be a good way to find out if it agrees with me. It obviously agrees with you. Elton told me a little of your background."

"Before we go any further, Miss Blaylock, shall we drop the formalities? May I call you Carrie?"

"Certainly. What do you prefer to be called?" Carrie wondered if he used a shorter name. Not "Mort," she thought. That sounds like death.

"I go by Morton." He didn't say anything for a few seconds, but Carrie sensed he wanted to. "My wife tried to come up with a suitable nickname, thought Morton was too … I don't know, stuffy or something. But I insisted on Morton."

"Well if it was good enough for your wife, it should be good enough for me … Morton," said Carrie, smiling.

Olivia returned with a pot of tea and three cups and explained that Elton was out for a bit but had said for them to start without him. She poured the tea and took a seat. "I've warned Morton about you, Carrie," Olivia said, lowering the cup from her lips.

"Warned him?" said Carrie, slightly embarrassed.

"You're the smartest and best-read woman he's ever likely to encounter, and I don't want him to feel intimidated."

Carrie wanted to appear as professional as possible on this the first step on what could be a life-long path. She felt herself blushing.

"You should know me well enough, Cousin, to know that I'm not intimidated by smart women," Morton said. "I was, after all, married to one. Now, coquettish or flirtatious women, that's another story."

Carrie relaxed and gave him a warm smile. "Well then, Morton, you certainly have nothing to fear from me."

***

Carrie lay in bed that night with a level of satisfaction she hadn't felt in … how long? She couldn't remember. The discussions with Morton, and Elton after he returned, couldn't have gone better from her standpoint. The three of them, with Olivia looking on, agreed that they would open a school. Morton would be the headmaster and teach the boys. Carrie would be his assistant and teach the girls. There was much to be worked out before they could enroll their first student, like finding a suitable building. They all agreed that it was hopeless while Rosecrans's army was still camped around Murfreesboro, but that would end any day now. After fixing up a building, they would need books and other supplies. It seemed like an overwhelming task, but Carrie felt sure that Morton, with Elton's help, was up to it. If things went as planned, she'd be teaching girls in September.

***

Morton Walling had asked if he might escort Carrie home, and with only the slightest hesitation, she consented. This was going to be an association to treasure, she could tell. There was so much to learn from him.

The conversation on their walk quickly turned personal. Carrie knew that he had a daughter, but didn't know her name—Dorthea—and didn't know her age—five. Morton's wife had died of typhoid fever, Carrie knew from Olivia, but hadn't heard when—not long after he left for the war. He hadn't even been able to return for the funeral. He'd been home only once since her death, the summer before when Bragg moved his Confederate army across Alabama to Chattanooga. Carrie fought back tears as Morton spoke movingly of his longing to be with Dorthea.

"So you won't go back to Alabama to live?"

"I have no family there. I'll need help raising a daughter. It's either here or back to North Carolina. I'm here, so I might as well stay."

"But you have your in-laws, they're keeping your daughter."

"It will be an adjustment for Dorthea leaving them, but …" he paused. "There are issues."

Home for Morton Walling was Tuscaloosa, where he'd relocated to become headmaster of a new school. He was originally from North Carolina, attended the university at Chapel Hill, and was teaching in Raleigh when the opportunity to head the school in Alabama presented itself. Morton arrived there a bachelor in his thirties with no thought of ever taking a wife. But that changed when he met Virginia Grant at a church function not long after she returned from Baltimore where she'd finished her schooling. Morton was thirty-two when they married.

Carrie hurriedly did the math; that made him now thirty-eight. Four years shy of twice her age.

As they approached the Blaylocks' house through the orchard, Morton stopped dead in his tracks. "What's that?" he asked, pointing with his good arm to the side of the house. "That flag, it looks like a regiment or brigade flag, a Federal one."

"We have a boarder, a staff officer with a Yankee brigade. We've been harassed by soldiers, and he hopes that by displaying the flag, whoever comes will think it's a headquarters like so many other houses, and they'll leave us alone."

"So you have a Yankee officer living with you?"

"A boarder, as I said."

"I'll leave you here if you don't mind."

"I don't think he's here now, if that's a problem."

"I'll keep my distance just the same." He'd been looking toward the house, but turned to Carrie. "I've run my mouth about myself all the way from town, and I'd like to know more about you."

Carrie broke into a smile. "There isn't much to know, Morton. I've led a fairly sheltered life."

"For the past two years you haven't."

"That's certainly true. Will you be at Olivia and Elton's Wednesday?"

"Will you?"

"I can be, after our reading circle."

"Then I shall be as well."

***

That night, John returned to the Blaylocks' by the light of the moon after everyone was in bed. Carrie could hardly wait to see him the next morning and give him the news. "I couldn't ask for anything more," she said over her shoulder while she mixed the milk into the cornmeal. "If we can make this work, I'll not only be teaching, but teaching under someone who I have so much to learn from. He's been doing this all his adult life."

"It sounds like a fine opportunity to see if you like it."

"I've thought of that." Carrie wiped her hands on her apron and turned to face him. "You know, John, we've had this discussion several times about my future, but we've never discussed yours. What do you see for yourself after the war? I mean, other than getting married?"

"Restart my law practice and perhaps get into politics. At least that's what I'd assumed. Now, though, I'm not so sure. So many of my ideas don't seem to be holding up. But I'm happy for you, Carrie, the opportunity to work with this man. I just regret that I won't be around to see you in the classroom. Like that prickly pear cactus that'll bloom in the glade after we're gone."

"Yes, like the cactus," she said, forcing a smile and turning back to the stove.

***

John rode away that morning as usual, and again that night he wasn't back by the time Carrie climbed the stairs to her room. She expected to see him the next morning, but he hadn't returned in the night. He didn't show up at all that day or the next, but the following evening while sitting alone on the porch, she saw him riding up the lane in the approaching twilight.

He joined her on the porch but hardly said a word. Something was troubling him, she could tell. She wondered if he'd finally gotten into it with one of the officers on the other side of the emancipation question. The passing months since the effective date of President Lincoln's proclamation hadn't dimmed the passion of those with strongly held opinions, and that included John. He'd shared with Carrie the threats he'd received, some veiled, some not so veiled, and it didn't help that he was a staff officer, which branded him as a "sissy" in the eyes of some men.

Carrie beat back her urge to ask John if something was wrong. After a long silence, he finally spoke up.

"This whole endeavor seemed so clear to me."

"Endeavor?"

"Putting down the rebellion, the war. It was such an obvious choice between right and wrong, between good and evil."

"And?"

"Now I'm not so sure."

His division had been sent out on an expedition into the no-man's land between the Federal picket lines and the hills protecting the Confederate army. No one knew for sure the purpose of the move, but General Bradley suspected that it was to probe the Rebel defenses in anticipation of the coming campaign.

The countryside was devastated. Houses were burned to the ground, and some families were living in barns, some even in chicken coops. Emaciated women and children wandered to the roadside begging for food, many of them dressed in rags. Only a few children wore shoes. As John rode with General Bradley along a road through some woods, they heard a commotion off to their right. Straining to listen, it sounded like a woman screaming. "Go see what that's all about," the brigadier told John.

Riding up a narrow track into the woods in the direction of the noise, John rounded a bend and came upon a squad of soldiers in front of a cabin next to a cleared field. When he got closer, he saw a young woman holding a baby. "I don't have enough experience to know how old the child is," John said to Carrie, "but I'd guess maybe one." Two little barefoot girls clung to their mother's dress, or what was left of a dress. Then as he got closer, John saw the source of the disturbance. In the middle of the soldiers stood a bony man in the butternut brown of a Confederate private.

John dismounted and approached the Union sergeant. "What's this all about?"

"Our orders are to take in any Johnnies we come across, and his wife's pitching a fit over it," the sergeant said.

"Don't take him, Captain, please don't take him. We'll starve if you do." The woman started crying, but wasn't as riled up as she sounded earlier. She wasn't screaming.

"Those are our orders, Captain," repeated the sergeant, "but sir, it don't seem right. This pitiful boy says he was conscripted into Wheeler's cavalry and now he's through with the army."

"I'm not one to disobey orders, Sergeant," John replied.

The woman sat the child she was holding on the ground and rushed John. Falling to her knees, she wrapped her arms around his legs. "Please, Captain, I beg you," she cried. "Don't take him. He never had a mind to be in no army to begin with. They made him. He won't ever again fight. I promise."

John's heart thumped in his chest as he pondered what to do. "We have our orders, ma'am."

"Think of these little children," she said looking up at him, her tears leaving streaks down her dirty face.

John stalled while trying to decide what to do. "Sergeant, you take the men back to the road. I'll bring the Johnnie in by myself." John unfastened his holster and pulled out his revolver. He cocked it. "Get away from me!" The young woman released her grip and fell back onto her heels. He backed away from her and aimed his revolver at the Confederate deserter. "You stay put, Reb." John waited with his revolver pointed at the boy while the other men marched back to the road, out of his sight.

John paused in recounting the story and looked at Carrie with sad eyes. "It could have been me who killed your brother or your intended."

Carrie's voice quivered. "But you weren't at Mill Springs or Shiloh."

"Figuratively, I mean, not literally." He thought for a minute. "You know, Carrie, that boy's not some wealthy slave-owning cotton planter. He's just struggling to feed and clothe his family, yet it's boys like him we're trying to whip. They're the ones who make up the Rebel army."

They were quiet for a minute before Carrie spoke. "So what happened to the boy, the deserter, did you take him in?"

"Of course I did. Those were our orders." They were again silent before John spoke. "But the boy got away from me as I was leading him back to the road."

***

Lying in her bed that night, Carrie was aware, strangely for the fist time, that John lay in his bed only a few steps from her. As she pictured him there in her father's study, her mind drifted to the woman he would be sharing his bed with. I wonder, she thought, does the girl appreciate what a thoroughly decent man she's marrying? Carrie didn't know why she felt this way, but for some reason, she didn't think the girl did fully appreciate John. An idea popped up. Write Miranda a letter. Inform her how terribly kind her fiancé had been to all of them during the army's stay at Murfreesboro. Remind her that she's marrying an intelligent, compassionate, sensitive man and tell her that she should be grateful. Carrie would never again lay eyes on John Lockridge after the army marched away, as it would any day now, and she'd never meet Miranda Escobar—Miranda Lockridge—but for some reason she didn't comprehend, it was important that John's future wife appreciate his qualities, traits she might not have found in another man.

Carrie lit the candle, reached for the Bible, and turned it to Psalm 30.

I will extol thee, O Lord; for thou hast lifted me up,
and hast not made my foes to rejoice over me.

***

Carrie and Olivia Stephenson left The Circle the next Wednesday walking together toward the square.

"Did Morton tell you we're meeting again today at your house?"

"No, but he's always welcome. *Almost* always."

Observing Olivia's sly grin, Carrie felt a twitch deep within her and a slight flush sweeping over her cheeks. "We're having another planning session," Carrie said, conscious that she was stretching the meaning of "planning session."

When they reached the house, Olivia left Carrie and Morton alone.

"Morton, perhaps we could start our search for a suitable building even before Rosecrans's army moves out. John thinks that he might be able to find some ranking officer who'll help us."

"John?"

"He's met General Thomas a few times and offered to do what he can to help."

"John who?"

"Oh, I'm sorry, I thought you knew. He's our boarder."

"The officer? You've been talking to him about our school?"

"Is that a problem?"

Morton looked away for an instant before he spoke. "I suppose not. It's not my place to dictate who you talk to."

"I'm pleased to hear you say that. And besides, he's an educated man like you. He attended Kenyon College in Ohio. I do respect his opinion."

"You may not want to share that with your reading friends."

"I've got better sense than to do that."

The time got away as Carrie lost herself in conversation. They'd started out discussing the school, as usual, but as usual, the talk drifted, and she offered what little there was to share about her life. When she told him of the loss of her father, the loss of her brother, and of the loss of the man she thought she'd marry and saw his eyes glisten with tears, she struggled to hold back her own.

"I must be getting home. I do have responsibilities."

"I'd like for us to get together more often than on Wednesdays," Morton said. "What about you?"

Carrie's mind shot back to February and Major Hobson's surprise invitation to the concert. She was more careful this time. "I'd like that."

"It may seem childish, but until your boarder leaves, I wouldn't feel comfortable calling at your house. Can we meet here at Olivia's?"

"Of course. When?"

"Day after tomorrow?"

"I'll plan on being here at noon."

***

Carrie was relieved Morton hadn't come to the house. He seemed to have a strong aversion to encountering a Yankee officer, and John was sitting with a book on the front porch.

"I'm surprised to find you here in the middle of the day," said Carrie, pulling a chair next to his.

"It's deathly quiet in camp; nothing but endless drilling."

"What are you reading?"

"You keep talking about Dickens, so I thought I'd try the one you just finished with your group."

"Do you like it?"

"I haven't gotten too far into it."

"So you haven't been here long?"

"Actually I have. I've had a long talk with Cassie."

"Cassie? About what?"

"Her life. Honestly, Carrie, you could make it into a novel."

"She must have told you how she got here."

Cassie had related that she grew up in the next county on the Johnson place near Triune. At about age fifteen, she took up with her "man" as she called him, and they had a son together. The master named him Sampson, hoping he would grow up to be strong. When Johnson fell on hard times and needed cash, he sold her man south. She still wasn't over it, she related to John. Sometime later, a house servant girl told Cassie she'd overheard Mr. and Mrs. Johnson arguing about selling Sampson south. Mrs. Johnson was dead set against taking the boy away from his mother, but Mr. Johnson said they desperately needed the money, and Sampson would fetch a good price. At least that's what Cassie was told. So she took her son and ran off. She picked her way through the countryside at night unsure where she was headed, hiding out in the daytime, and somehow made it to the Stones River.

"Starved and half naked," Carrie said. "My brother found them on the riverbank." She explained that this was about the time Uncle Edward had passed and left the place to her parents. Her father let Cassie and Sampson move into the old slave cabin. The farm hadn't been kept up in Uncle Edward's later years, and in exchange for a place to live, Cassie and Sampson went to work getting it back in order. To all the world they appeared to be the Blaylocks' slaves.

"So your family has never owned a slave?"

"Father wouldn't hear of it."

"But you told me that you were spoiled by not having to work around the house."

"We had paid help, free blacks mostly, but sometimes white girls from the country. That felt, how shall I put it, uncomfortable, those girls, some my own age, cooking and cleaning up after me. But …"

"But what?"

"I didn't feel that way about the colored girls."

"Isn't that inconsistent with not having slaves?"

"I don't think so. I mean, holding firmly to the belief that one human being shouldn't own another is not the same as believing everyone is equal."

"So you don't believe Negroes are equal?"

"If I didn't, I certainly wouldn't be in a minority, North or South. Don't come down here and tell me that in Columbus, Ohio, blacks are on equal footing with whites. How do you feel about it?"

"Being a lawyer, 'equal' means under the law, and yes, everyone should be treated equally."

"Do you mean socially as well? Or are Negroes inferior like most people presume?"

"I can't say. How about you?"

"I've thought about it, I really have. The way I see it, Sampson's as intelligent as most white people I know. Perhaps if he'd had the advantages you and I've had, there wouldn't be any difference. But I don't know that. Look at Dickens, the way he portrayed England. That society is hardly one in which people are treated equally, and their race has nothing to do with it. It's just assumed that certain people will have a higher station in life. Ultimately, in America, North or South, it'll depend on education. Those who are educated will get ahead. That will be more important than a person's race."

"I suppose that figures into your passion for teaching."

"It certainly does. I have the benefit of an education, and so do you. I'd like to see everyone have that benefit."

"Does that include the coloreds?"

"It certainly does."

"Will you be taking coloreds into your new school?"

"We haven't discussed it, but I shouldn't think so."

"That seems inconsistent, don't you think?"

"They can have their own schools. I'm sure you've heard about the Northern missionaries coming here to start schools for them. I don't hear about them starting schools for white children."

"No."

Neither of them spoke for a while.

"Do you have any news about when you … the army will be leaving?"

"Nothing but the same old rumors. The president and General Halleck in Washington are anxious for Rosecrans to do something."

"I can't stand the thought of another battle, but I suppose it's inevitable. It is war, after all."

"Our boys are restless. The sooner we fight, the sooner it'll be over, the sooner we can all go home."

***

"He's in the back room," said a sergeant when John inquired about Captain Goodman. He was at the office of the army's provost marshal in a storefront just off the Courthouse Square.

"Fetch him for me if you would," said John, fidgeting with the handle of his officer's sword while he waited.

Goodman emerged from the back room. "Lockridge, what brings you here?"

"I have some information that may be useful to you."

"About the two bodies?"

"I assume you're still looking into it."

"Truthfully, I haven't had much time. We've been busy processing captured Johnnies. And our own deserters."

"That's what I want talk to you about. After you visited our brigade, I got curious and started checking around. I believe the two men deserted from the 78th Pennsylvania in our division."

"Why do you say that?"

John explained that because his division was camped closest to where Goodman thought the men had been shot, he sought out information from his counterparts in the other brigades. The Third Brigade adjutant reported that two men from the Western Pennsylvania regiment had gone missing just after payday, right around the time it was believed they were shot. From the regimental adjutant, John learned that the two men had been vocal about not wanting to fight alongside the colored infantry that was being organized. The regiment had reported the men missing.

"I did see two men missing from that regiment on the daily report, now that you mention it, but there are so many now, I didn't think much of it. So I guess they were deserters as you suspected."

"That's the way I see it."

Goodman asked if it would be safe to put that conclusion in a report to Major Wiles, the provost marshal. "That should be the end of it, regardless of how they got themselves killed. I mean, if they were on the run."

"Then you won't need to question the widow or her family?"

"I don't see any need to now."

It was a relief, but still, John felt nervous. "You're welcome to quote me in your report."

"That won't be necessary. Thanks for your follow-up, and if I can ever do anything for you, let me know."

***

Like all soldiers, John Lockridge took comfort in mail from home and was careful to reciprocate by being a faithful correspondent. His mother, in her most recent letter, related that Miranda had been to see her asking about him. Had something happened? It had been a while since Miranda had received a letter. His mother wrote him that she'd told Miranda that nothing bad had happened as far as she knew.

John had been avoiding writing Miranda. And he'd been avoiding admitting it to himself. The last lines of his mother's letter knocked him off balance.

> *Are you so captivated by the widow's daughter that you've forgotten your obligation to your fiancée? You've mentioned the girl in every letter since you wrote to ask if by chance your father might have*

known hers. Whatever it is, son, you owe Miranda an explanation. It's beneath you to cause her to suffer.

***

Carrie awoke in the night feeling slightly nauseated. Her room was heavy and suffocating in the early summer heat, so she sought cooler air on the porch. With her shawl draped over her shoulders, she felt her way down the stairs.

"Oh!" she exclaimed. John was sitting in one of the rockers.

"I couldn't sleep." He stood to greet her.

Carrie hurriedly clutched her shawl around her. She felt a bit wobbly on her feet, and turned to go back upstairs.

"Please join me," John said.

She paused to consider the decency of it before taking the chair closest to him. Neither of them spoke for a few seconds.

"Something's wrong, isn't it?" she asked.

"You're getting to know me pretty well." He took a deep breath. "I thought I had it figured out, my life that is. Now I don't know. I feel … how to put it, out of kilter?" He glanced at her. "Sound's familiar, doesn't it?"

She looked into the darkness for a few seconds. "My sister-in-law, Martha, shared that she'd found relief from the crushing uncertainty by just allowing it, quit fighting it. When she did, she felt some peace."

"Has it worked for you?"

"Sometimes. It's better than the alternative: constantly fretting."

"My mind's such a jumble of thoughts and emotions, I wouldn't know what to quit fighting."

Carrie thought for a second, and then reached out her left hand and took his right hand. The sensation of their warm flesh touching brought the awareness of how alone they were. There wasn't the tiniest whiff of wind, and the still of the night was broken only by sounds of crickets and katydids.

And their own breathing. The fluttering of her heart settled down, and she lost track of time.

"John, go to bed." She'd noticed his head falling forward to his chest.

He jerked up, looked at her in a confused daze, rose, and walked into the house.

But not before pressing his lips to the hand that had stilled him.

***

Something pushed Carrie to try to look her best for her meetings with Morton, even if it did invite stares from the soldiers. So for each visit, she selected a colorful summer dress from the mahogany wardrobe in the corner of her room. This day, Friday, she wore her soft yellow muslin. Carrie had been working up to asking Morton to educate her about the business side of operating a school, and when she did, a puzzled expression swept across his face.

"Why?"

"I want to know everything you have to teach me."

"But women don't concern themselves with business matters."

His response left her tongue-tied for an instant. "Forgive my boldness, Morton, but I've grown intolerant of prejudice against my sex. I *will* learn about the business of running a school, if not from you then from someone else."

His gaze lingered on her for what seemed like forever. "My, you are different," he said, opening a spontaneous, affirming grin.

A satisfied smile crossed Carrie's lips. She'd been scheming for months about making her own way in life and wasn't about to settle for one choked by convention.

It turned out to be her most enjoyable time so far with Morton Walling.

***

The following Wednesday, Carrie struck out early for The Circle to stop by the post office. Lizzy Forbes had vowed to make her decision by early May, and Carrie was anxious to learn it, though she was fairly certain what it would be. The letter was waiting.

Sunday, May 17, '63

My Dearest Friend,

I've taken your advice and told Gunter "yes." You're right, why put it off if it's what I want. Now the question is "when?" He didn't press me. It's comforting to think of having Mother and Papa around when I become a mother as opposed to being away from them in Cincinnati, I suppose. But it seems like such a dreadful time to bring a helpless infant into this world. Wouldn't we be better off waiting? But how long will we have to wait?

He suggested a quick trip to Cincinnati to meet his parents and his son. I'm excited but also apprehensive. What if the boy doesn't like me?

The more hopeful tone of your letters warms my heart. Your friendship with Captain Lockridge must be agreeing with you. I'm glad you don't feel so lonely now. Keep me posted on the school plans. I trust you're still impressed with the headmaster. From what you say, he must be a solid man.

I must stop. I hope you're excited about my news. Maybe I'll be hearing some from you before long.

Your loyal and best friend,
Lizzy

***

Leaving The Circle, Carrie took advantage of her time alone with Olivia Stephenson to ask about what might be in store for Lizzy, being a mother to another woman's child.

"I hardly think of them as someone else's boys. Oh, every now and then it arises in my consciousness, mostly sorrow for their mother who I hardly knew. And, I suspect that there's a mother-child bond that can't be replaced or duplicated."

Carrie related that she'd just found out that Lizzy accepted the marriage proposal from the army surgeon and was curious what she could expect.

"Children want mothers more than anything, and from what you've told me about her, the boy couldn't ask for a better one." Olivia stopped and clasped Carrie by the arm. "Could there be more to it, more to your question?"

"Like what?"

"Morton."

"Morton?"

"He's taken a fancy to you, or haven't you noticed?"

Carrie's mind shot to the image she'd been seeing lately, of a little girl in desperate need of a mother, a beautiful five-year-old, of tying ribbons in hair for Sunday church and of reading to her at bedtime. She fished for the right response. "I'm not too observant about … you know, male-female relations." A factual statement as far as it went. In truth, she was conscious of a deepening connection between her and Morton. But she was unsure of the exact nature of it.

"Now that you know, what are your feelings about it?"

"Flattered I suppose."

"Is that all?"

"It's difficult to explain," said Carrie, warming up to repeat the same lines she'd given John about living independently, "but the life I've decided upon doesn't include a man, at least not in the conventional sense."

"From my vantage point, your relationship with Morton hardly seems conventional."

"No, I guess it's not."

"Can I give you some advice?"

"Of course."

"This cruel war will end someday, and when it does you may wish you weren't alone. Think of all the solitary meals, of never awaking in the arms of a man who desires you, of the poverty of a life without the laughter of children."

"I've thought of all that and more."

"Then stay open to possibilities. We don't know how God's plan will unfold. I'm living proof of it."

***

Every morning Captain Lockridge rode to brigade headquarters expecting something different. President Lincoln's desire to liberate East Tennessee's Unionist majority bordered on an obsession, so it was said, and rumors were as thick as the flies that he was on the verge of ordering Rosecrans to move toward Chattanooga at once or be relieved of command. But each day was not much different from the one before.

The captain had saddled his horse one morning and was about to mount when he spotted Sarah Blaylock hustling toward him, her pretty face brightened by the soft morning sun. The usually carefree girl presented a look of intensity he'd not seen in her.

"I need to talk to you," she said in a low voice, looking up at him.

"About what?"

"Not here. Can I walk with you up to the pike?"

He'd noticed lately that whenever Sarah sought him out, Carrie usually showed up and joined them. He was rarely alone with the girl.

"Sure. I'd love your company." The captain held the rein in his right hand and started down the lane through the orchard with Sarah on his left. After they were out of sight of the house, a pleasurable sensation startled him. She slid her hand down the inside of his left arm and then gripped his rough hand tightly in hers. He gave her a quick look, but her eyes were focused straight ahead. They took a few hand-in-hand strides before she spoke.

"I know you love my sister."

He felt like he'd been struck by a bolt of lightning.

"I've seen the letters."

He wrestled for a response as they kept walking. "Letters?"

"In your room."

He stopped and pulled away.

"You've been snooping through my possessions?"

Sarah faced him and reminded him that in the wartime division of labor her mother had decreed, it was her job to clean the house, and that included the study where he slept. "The letters are in plain sight. First there was one, then a second, and now a third—three letters from your fiancée you haven't even opened."

"And you know they're from her, do you? You've studied the return address?"

"I can tell by the color, light blue, not like the ones from your family."

"I see," he said, unsure what to say next. "Perhaps there's some explanation you don't know about, Sarah. There could be several."

"I may not be as old as you, but I know more about some things than you think I do. There can be only one reason for not opening her letters. You've fallen for someone else."

They looked each other in the eyes.

"I suppose you've told your mother?"

"I haven't told anyone, and I don't intend to. It's between you and me."

"That's at least some good news."

Sarah drew her lips together and focused her gaze at him. "I don't want my sister to get hurt, you understand?"

"Sarah, I wouldn't do anything to hurt any of you."

"You wouldn't on purpose, I know that. But Carrie's not like most others her age. She's not … how can I say it? She's not as aware about some things."

"I don't know what else I can say."

"You don't have to say anything. I just wanted to talk to you about it, that's all."

Her face relaxed, and he was shocked by the arousing sensation of her lips kissing his cheek.

"Have a safe day, Captain."

***

That evening Carrie and John took advantage of the long day to follow the path out to the bluff before darkness fell. "Hold on," he said as they entered the rocky glade.

She followed him to the prickly pear cactus. "Any day now," she said.

"Too long for me," he replied flatly, staring down.

Carrie said nothing as they walked on to the gazebo. She took her usual seat. But John didn't. He put himself down on her section of the bench, close enough for her to sense his thigh pressing against hers, close enough for her to feel a quickening inside.

Her chest tightened. Had the moment arrived that would catapult her back into punishing loneliness? John had been updating her on preparations for the coming campaign. Amidst much grumbling, the army had issued two-man "dog tents" to lighten the load for the march. Rosecrans had decreed that all officers reduce their baggage and ship excess back to Nashville. Just that morning the men were ordered to fill their haversacks with five days' rations. And it was the end of May, way past the time President Lincoln—and everyone else—expected Rosecrans to strike.

This is like waiting for the other shoe to drop, she thought. A turbulent silence stretched between them.

The deep croak of a bullfrog and the ripple of the river were the only sounds until Carrie spoke. "What shall we read when we finish this," she said, holding up *Ivanhoe*, hoping for a response that would say that her friend's departure wasn't so imminent.

"Whatever you say."

His air of resignation only heightened her apprehension.

The sun sinking in the west filled the sky with a bright pink while they passed the book back and forth. When darkness was about to shut them off from the rest of the world, they walked in silence to the house and disappeared into their separate rooms.

***

Something was not right. The fire burned in the stove, the coffee was boiled, but there was no sign of John. Carrie peered through the open door of the study. He wasn't there. She went to the parlor. No John. She rushed to the front porch. "John!" The roar of heavy rain on the roof was the only sound until a clap of thunder made her jump. He wouldn't go out in this, she thought, unless he had to. Or unless something's happened to him.

She returned to the kitchen, took the milk pail, and then dashed through the curtain of water to the barn and into Milk Cow's stall. "Oh!" she exclaimed as she set down the pail. John came out of the shadows.

"You startled me." Her voice barely carried above the din of the rain. Something was different about him. His face had a distressed look she hadn't seen before. Or had she?

"What's her name; you've never told me," he said.

"Who's name?"

"The cow."

What an odd time for this question, Carrie thought. She felt her shoulders tighten. "Milk Cow, just Milk Cow. We never got around to giving her a name."

They stood with their eyes fixed on each other, almost like strangers meeting for the first time, until she turned her back to him to pick up the milking stool. But before she could, he grabbed her from behind and tightened his arms around her.

"John, what are you doing?"

"Be quiet."

"What's gotten into you? Let me go!" She wanted to scream, but the heavy rain drumming on the shingled roof would drown it out.

"Carrie, be still. Just be still."

She wiggled, or tried to, but he clasped his arms around her midsection, pinning her arms to her side. She squirmed until her shoulders slumped in exhausted submission. He turned her to face him, keeping a loose grip on her arms above her elbows. She saw that his eyes were glossy.

"Carrie, there's something I have to tell you."

Her head swam with possibilities.

"All I live for is our time together. Nothing else matters to me anymore, not the cause for which I fight, not anyone else. Nothing."

Her fright eased enough to force a few words. "You're a lonely soldier."

"Lonely when I'm not with you." He relaxed his grip.

"John, you're committed to another woman."

"You're the only one I care about, Carrie. You must believe me."

The thunder of her heartbeat was so loud that even the roar of the rain on the roof couldn't muffle it. She felt it in her head, too, the throbbing.

"Tell me you don't feel the same, and I'll ride away this moment, and you'll never have to see me again."

Her stomach twisted into a knot. "I can't bear the thought of it."

His voice softened. "Then tell me you think of me as much as I think of you."

"I try not to."

"But you do, don't you?"

She looked away, but his hand touched her chin and turned her face back to him. She was helpless to stop the tears streaking down her freckled cheeks. He pulled her to him and gently stroked her hair. The wool of his coat tickled her face, and the scent of wood smoke in his wet uniform took her mind back to the bluff, to when they had sat so close, when she had secretly longed for the refuge of his arms.

***

This is the longest day of my life, Carrie thought later that day. The storm had cleansed the air of thickness, leaving behind a crisp, cloudless early summer day. A slight chill emerged after the sun slid behind the trees. Sitting alone on the porch, she wrapped her shawl around her and focused her eyes on the lane. Whether John would return this night, she didn't know. She never did. But she did know one thing for certain. After she said what had to be said, she'd never again lay eyes on him. She labored to still her mind, to try to embrace rather than resist her sadness over the end of their friendship.

That morning there had been none of their usual playful banter in the kitchen. Carrie forced herself to eat what little she could at breakfast, and the two of them hardly spoke. Her mother stared at Carrie and then stared at John. Something had changed.

After John left for camp and she finished her morning chores, Carrie went to the bluff to think, to pray. Her mind whirled in different directions until she finally settled on a course of action. The disappointment stung her heart, but it was her only rational choice. She returned to the house with her decision.

***

Carrie thought her heart would burst three days later when she saw John riding up the lane in the approaching twilight. "Where've you been?" she called out. "I've been worried."

He didn't reply, and rode on to the barn. She was on edge when he took a chair next to her on the porch.

"General Thomas insists that his corps be ready to leave on a moment's notice, and he means that literally. That takes work. But let's not talk of war. I just want to be with you. My only hope is that you feel the same."

Carrie felt tears threatening. "Let's go to the bluff, shall we?"

He followed her down the narrow path through the cedars and into the glade. When she turned to start up the little rise into the hardwoods, John was no longer behind her. She paused, but when he didn't show himself, she walked back into the rocky opening. He was standing over the prickly pear cactus.

"Remember when you first showed me this?" he called out.

She couldn't get out a single word when she reached him.

"Well I do," he said. "I told you then that I didn't know where I'd be when it bloomed, but I knew it wouldn't be here. Well, here I am." He looked down at the yellow flower before looking back at her. "I can see why you like it so much."

When he followed her into the gazebo, he sat close to her, like the last time.

Carrie's heart pounded in her chest as she worked to summon the will to say what had to be said. As much as anything, she was afraid of how he'd take it.

"John, I've been thinking about the other morning, and ..."

"Same here, and I'm relieved you're here with me."

He doesn't have a clue, she thought. She turned toward him, grasped his right hand, and squeezed it in both of hers. "You've been such a good friend. I can't ... I've never felt this close to anyone. But I don't see any possibility ... I mean, you'll be leaving any day, and ... I'm so confused."

"Are you?"

"Yes. I mean, no. But it's just that I can't envision … this horrid war, it seems destined to drag on forever."

"And you fear you'll never see me again."

"That's possible, isn't it?"

"Not if I'm alive."

"But …"

"I can't force you to believe me, Carrie."

"I trust you, John. It's not that. It's just that so much is out of our control." She took a deep but shaky breath to steady herself and force the lines she'd been rehearsing over and over for two days. Tears stung her eyes. She rested her head on his shoulder to gain her composure. Believing she could say what had to be said, she pushed away and opened her eyes to meet his.

"I … John … Oh John," she whimpered, folding her arms around his waist.

CHAPTER SIX

June 1863

"So, Carrie, how is it these days with that Yankee captain? I assume he's still boarding at your place?" asked Cat Bonds at the first gathering of The Circle in June.

Carrie felt a rush of alarm. "Uneventful," she said, praying her voice wouldn't crack.

"Find out from him what Rosecrans is planning for the next campaign so we can get word of it to our boys."

They all turned to Carrie.

"He's just a captain."

"But he's a brigade staff officer. He's bound to hear talk," Cat shot back.

"I doubt that I could persuade him to share any military secrets even if I wanted to," said Carrie, feeling the urge to bolt from the gathering. "He seems to be a rather straight-laced fellow."

"Flirt with him if you have to," Kate said with a laugh.

Carrie could still feel John's hand pressing against the small of her back, melding them together that morning as they kissed in the seclusion of the barn. She replied as stone-faced as she could manage: "You know flirting's not my strong suit."

"Oh, for goodness sake, Carrie, loosen up for once in your life," said Kate, still laughing.

Carrie cast a pleading glance at her sister-in-law.

"Let's return to our book," Martha said.

***

Carrie and Olivia left together as usual, but before they reached the Square, Carrie stopped. "Go on without me. I need to go back to discuss something with Martha. Family business, you know. Tell Morton I'll be along directly." She whirled around and hustled in the opposite direction.

Martha had retrieved little David from upstairs by the time Carrie returned, and when the boy spotted his aunt, he toddled to her with arms raised. She lifted him, gave him a kiss on his chubby cheek, and planted him on her hip. "You've figured it out, haven't you," Carrie said to Martha.

"It's been apparent for some time, to me at least."

"I've been mortally afraid of what you'll think of me."

"I hope I can speak to you frankly and honestly."

"Certainly."

"I'm having difficulty envisioning a happy ending."

"I tried to say no."

"We can't control our emotions."

"I'm learning that."

"But we can control our behavior."

***

Morton was not at Olivia's when Carrie arrived. "You got away so fast that I didn't get the chance to tell you," Olivia said. "Morton's gone."

"Gone?"

"He's trying to get to Tuscaloosa to get to Dorthea."

"How did he get outside the Federal lines?"

It was all very mysterious, Olivia reported, but as best she could determine, Morton had made the acquaintance of a provost marshal officer who'd issued him a pass. Goodman, she thought the man's name was. Carrie replied that he was the officer who'd issued her the pass for her Nashville trip back in February and asked Olivia how Morton had made the acquaintance. Morton seemed so steadfast in his aversion to encountering any Yankee officers. Olivia didn't know.

"What are his plans if he makes it to Dorthea?" Carrie asked.

"I'm not sure he thought it through that far. He's focused right now on just getting there."

"Then he might not return?"

"Oh no, he'll return as quickly as he can. He's committed to your project, quite excited about the school. He didn't tell me this, but I'm sure he has no thought of abandoning his intentions toward you either. He left this for you." Olivia picked up an envelope from the low table.

Carrie recognized Morton's clumsy left-hand scrawl. "I'll read it when I'm alone if you don't mind."

"Of course," said Olivia with a twinkle in her eye.

***

Carrie greeted the news about Morton with a dissonant mix of thoughts and emotions. She was relieved that she'd be freed, for a while at least, from her niggling suspicion that she was treating Morton as a card to hold and play should any of the unhappy options with John come to pass. At the same time, Carrie was sad over the news. She'd grown accustomed to Morton's companionship. And however optimistic he was about a quick return, she knew that wouldn't happen. The widespread chaos meant that it was unlikely he'd make it back in time to get the school open by September. She was afraid for Morton as well. North Alabama, with its conflicting loyalties, was as lawless as Tennessee's Upper Cumberland, they'd all heard, and he'd have to travel through there to get down to Tuscaloosa. And back with a child in tow.

***

The last thing John Lockridge wanted was trouble with Carrie's mother. How much she knew about the two of them, he couldn't say, and if she did, whether she approved of it, he couldn't say either. But she did approve of him, of that he was certain. So he struggled with how to respond to Sampson's inquiry, fearful of how Amanda Blaylock would take it. There was no good answer.

The dilemma arose one evening as darkness started to fall and John was unsaddling his horse in the barn after a late return from camp. Sampson ambled in and asked if he might have a word.

"Sure," John said. "What's on your mind?"

"What do you know about the colored regiments being organized and how I might join up?"

"I don't know," John answered, and without even thinking about it, added, "but I can find out for you. By the way, how did you learn about the colored regiments? "

"I read the newspapers that you bring home and throw away after you're finished with them."

"So you can read?"

"With respect, Captain, I just said I read your newspapers."

"But I thought it was against the law down here to … how did you learn to read, Sampson?"

"Miss Carrie, sir, she taught me back before the war started."

Now, a few days later, John struggled over whether to track down information about the colored regiments and pass it on to Sampson. Mrs. Blaylock, the girls, Cassie, all four of them depended on him for the heavy work around the place, and he was so talented with his hands, he could fix most anything. And what would Cassie think about her only child going off to war? On the other hand, helping Negroes achieve self-determination was one of the causes that prompted John to volunteer in the first place. Who was he to decide for Sampson how he should live his life? Besides, the boy could find out about the colored troops on his own. He was smart and resourceful.

***

"Did you do it, did you ask him?" said Cat the following Wednesday at The Circle. They all turned to Carrie.

"He's gone."

"Gone?" said one of the others.

"He moved out a few days ago. Officers boarding in private homes were ordered to camp."

"That tells us something," Cat said. "Rosecrans must be planning on moving out soon."

"But we don't know in what direction," Kate said. "That's what would be so helpful to get to our army."

"I'm sorry I can't be of any help," said Carrie, forcing a stiff smile to try to cover her half-truth.

***

She still saw John. They connived most every day to rendezvous at the bluff. Carrie managed to suppress her desire to cuddle with him in broad daylight, and stayed the model of decorum she'd always been. The awareness of how it would turn her life inside out if anyone but Martha knew about them was seldom far from her consciousness. A hidden goodbye kiss in the glade was the only display of her deepening affection she permitted herself.

Lost in their reading and conversation, Carrie was content now to savor their moments together without struggling to figure out where it was headed. Each day was a life of its own. Each day could be their last together until—who knew when? Maybe forever. But as the days crept by, her dormant anxiety over an uncertain future flared up. Lurking in the back of her mind was the foreboding that John was deceiving himself about his intentions toward her. Would he still feel the same when his life returned to normal, as it surely would someday, when he was back home in Columbus? Carrie kept her trepidation tamped down as long as she could, but it finally boiled over. It was the second Saturday in June. She hungered for reassurance.

"Our discussions about a future together after the war haven't been idle conversation on my part," he protested.

"I know you believe that now, John, but what about later? Will you still feel the same when you're back home in familiar surroundings? Back in the presence of . . ."

"I can't state it any plainer."

Carrie leaned her head on his shoulder and took his hand. "I'm sorry. I'll work harder at being more trusting."

***

The next day, John was at the bluff when Carrie arrived. It was Sunday, and everyone else had gone to town. A warm gentle rain fell, and the steady tinkle of drops struck the cedar shakes on the gazebo roof. Mist rose from the river. They were alone in their own world, just the two of them. Casting off her protective shroud of propriety, Carrie wrapped her arms around him, raised her face to receive his kiss, and lost herself in their embrace.

It was only when she felt the length of John's body pressing hard against her that Carrie was conscious that she was lying on the narrow bench, powerless to halt his exploration. Under her dress, his calloused hands inched up her bare thigh. Goose bumps rose on the back of her neck, even as her face was on fire. With each throb of her heart, the words she'd heard at weddings pulsated in her head: "one flesh, one flesh, one flesh."

"No! I can't!" She bolted upright and knocked John onto the floor.

He looked up at her like a child who'd been scolded. Carrie instinctively extended her trembling hand. He accepted it and joined her sitting on the bench. They remained there, hand-in-hand in oppressive silence until he finally spoke.

"I must go."

When they reached their divergent paths in the glade, she leaned into him for their goodbye kiss, but he turned and strode toward the pike.

"Goodbye, Carrie." He didn't even look back at her.

***

Self-recriminating thoughts raced through Carrie's mind as she walked weak-kneed back to the house. How could I reject this man who so appreciates everything about me, who cares so much for me just the way I am?

Her mother had returned from town and was knitting on the front porch, sheltered from the rain. Carrie paused to try to compose herself and then without speaking passed her mother and climbed the stairs to her room. She undid the buttons of her wet dress, lifted it over her head, and set it aside to dry. She stretched out on the bed in her chemise, staring at the ceiling. The numbness of her mind was a relief.

There was a gentle knock on the door.

"Carrie?" It was her mother.

"What is it?"

"May I come in?"

"Yes," said Carrie, swinging her legs around to sit on the edge of her bed.

They sat in silence for a few minutes before Carrie finally spoke.

"You know, don't you, Mother?"

"Yes dear, I know."

"Oh, Mother," Carrie sniveled, "I didn't plan this. It just happened. I don't know what to do."

Amanda coddled her to her breast like when she was a little girl, stroking the back of her head. "All love involves pain sooner or later."

"I may never see him again."

"That's the way life is. One day someone you love is here, and the next day, they're gone."

"And if I do see him, I don't know how I'm supposed to behave. Our time together is so short."

"These are unprecedented times, my dear. The old rules don't fit anymore."

Carrie drew back, and wiping the tears from her face with the back of her hand, gave her mother an inquisitive look. "Are you suggesting that it's all right if I—"

"I'm not suggesting anything."

They looked each other in the eyes for a few seconds. "I only ask that you keep one thing in mind," her mother said.

"What?"

"There could be consequences."

***

Carrie sat alone at the bluff on a sweltering June day, dabbing her brow with her handkerchief. She'd come several days in a row hoping, praying, that John would return to her. Each day he didn't felt worse than the one before.

Her mind drifted back to when her father had died, to when lifelong friends turned on each other, and conflicting loyalties tore apart Tennessee. She'd thought then that she couldn't feel any worse. Then came war, the loss of her brother. And Grantland.

But take all of that, she thought, add it all up, and it doesn't match the pain burning in me over losing John. Then again, maybe it's for the best. Only a few weeks ago, at this very spot, she'd realized that every path with John would only lead to more heartache. If she'd stuck with her decision then, she wouldn't be in such a miserable state now. Saying goodbye then would have hurt, but nothing like this.

***

The next morning while finishing the breakfast cleanup, Carrie heard a voice she didn't recognize coming from the front of the house. She thought she'd heard the voice raised in anger, but when she reached the porch, no one seemed angry. Sarah was talking to a boy dressed in the blue uniform of a soldier.

"Here she is," said Sarah as Carrie came through the front door. "This is Private Mallory." Sarah glanced at her sister before looking back at the boy. "He has something for you."

"I'm an orderly on General Bradley's staff, ma'am, and the brigade adjutant gave me this with instructions to deliver it to you in person." He pulled an envelope from his coat and handed it to Carrie. "My instructions are to take back your written reply with me. There's no rush, ma'am," said the private, casting a shy but hopeful glance at Sarah.

"Have a seat, Private," said Carrie, pointing to one of the rocking chairs. "Sarah, bring the boy some water."

Carrie ignored Sarah's sigh and retreated to the parlor. Her heart pounded. She lowered herself onto the settee and stared at the letter. Her back was so rigid, it was painful. Deep down, she doubted that John would really go away without making any effort to get in touch with her. In her obsessing about it, she'd concluded there could only be one of two messages he'd send, and she'd already decided how she'd respond to each of them. Carrie tried to steady her hands with a few deep breaths. She cut open the envelope and then read the letter. It didn't take her long to compose her reply.

"Here you are," said Carrie, handing the boy the envelope when she returned to the porch.

"Is there any special message, ma'am?"

"Just my letter," she said in a voice so calm that it surprised her.

The boy didn't seem to want to leave, and Sarah didn't appear eager for him to go, so Carrie returned to the kitchen, leaving the two of them on the porch.

***

Consequences.

The following Sunday her mother's admonition flared in Carrie's mind each time she stabbed the shovel into the dirt. She was on her knees digging for buried treasure. After Nashville fell to the Yankees, Amanda had decreed that they would hide their silver service and jewelry. Cassie, who was well-schooled in hiding things, suggested they stash their possessions in bits and pieces in several locations. Carrie's jewelry box was beneath several inches of dirt in one of the barn's clean back stalls, the same one she retreated to after the awful incident with the deserters.

Feeling the bump of the shovel blade against the box, she scraped away enough dirt to pry it open. The handkerchief folded around her ring was just as she'd left it. With it stuffed securely in her dress pocket, Carrie tediously replaced the dirt and covered it with straw. Standing back to examine it, she couldn't detect any evidence of her excavation.

***

Sitting on the porch alone at noon that day, Carrie's mind trotted around a circuit of competing thoughts and emotions: doubt, joy, shame, fear, guilt. And foolishness. Straining to observe the lane through the orchard, she had the unwelcome notion that she might have made a complete fool of herself in the way she responded to John's letter. For all she knew, he'd laughed off her proposal, maybe even shared the joke with his good friend Marshall.

Then her body tightened. She saw a rider coming through the fruit trees. "It's him," she muttered out loud, unable to recall ever feeling so hopeful seeing another human being.

John didn't so much as glance in her direction as he rode past the porch toward the hitching post. The silence grated on her raw nerves, and the radiant smile that had graced her face vanished. When he climbed the steps, she rose to greet him with a strange mixture of tension and relief. She saw in his right hand the red leather-bound book.

"You look absolutely beautiful."

She'd pinched a bright red rose from the corner of the house and pinned it in her hair, still damp from the washing. Her wine-red, off-the-shoulder silk dress with short sleeves felt smooth and cool against her clean bare skin.

"Do you believe I'm a fool for suggesting this?" she said with a quiver.

He leaned in, kissed her cheek, and whispered in her ear. "Obviously I don't."

"And you want to go through with it?"

He pulled back. "Why else would I be here?"

"Father gave me this as a graduation gift. I've hardly ever worn it."

John took the ring and slipped it on his little finger. She moved next to him so that they stood side-by-side facing the orchard. "I've been to a few of these, but never paid much attention to how it goes," he said with a laugh.

"I never dreamed my own would be under these circumstances."

"Are you sure about this?" he asked in an unsteady voice.

"It was my idea."

"All right then." He opened his Book of Common Prayer, and they held it together as if they were in church singing out of the same hymnal.

"I believe the groom goes first:

> *'I John, take thee Carrie, to by my lawful wedded Wife, to have and to hold from this day forward, for better for worse, for richer for poorer, in sickness and in health, to love and to cherish, till death us do part, according to God's holy ordinance; and thereto I plight thee my troth."*

He laughed nervously.

"What's funny?"

"That word, 'troth,' I've never known what it means."

"It means pledge." Carrie tried to calm herself with a deep breath.

> *"I Carrie, take thee John, to be my lawful wedded husband, to have and to hold from this day forward, for better or worse, for richer for poorer, in sickness and in health, to love, cherish, and to …"*

"What's wrong?" he asked. She'd stopped reading.

"I'm not sure I like that, 'obey.' That's not exactly what I have in mind for us."

"I said it."

"No you didn't. It's not in the groom's vows."

He reread the groom's vows to himself. "You're right. You know, I've never noticed the difference. Just leave it out then."

"Thank you …

> " *… till death us do part, according to God's holy ordinance; and thereto I plight thee my troth."*

John took Carrie's left hand, but before he could slip the ring on her finger, she pulled her hand away and lifted her right hand. "I'll wear it on this hand for now."

"That's wise," he said. "Let's see." He fumbled with his prayer book. "Here it is:

> *"Those whom God has joined together let no one put asunder."*

"Amen."

They stood facing each other in an uncomfortable silence as if asking themselves "what now?"

"Come on," she said. Taking John by the hand, Carrie led him through the front door and up the stairs to her bedroom.

***

Three days later, on Wednesday, June 24th, the singing birds announced the dawn of a new day, and Carrie stirred from her slumber to an odd sensation. What was it? Rumbling was the best she could come up with to describe it. She threw back the sheet and flattened her hands on her belly. She didn't feel anything unusual. She'd never, in all her years, asked anyone what it would feel like. Not even Martha; not even her mother. She hadn't had any reason to. Coming into full alertness, she listened intently. The same rumble. Then it came to her. She'd heard the identical sound before, during the night of January 3rd. It was the sound of an entire army on the move.

CHAPTER SEVEN

July 1863

John Lockridge savored the early morning panorama. From the brigade's camp atop a hill near the foot of the Cumberland Plateau, he studied the green wall rising from patches of fog hovering over the verdant fields. Here, not far from Winchester, Tennessee, the Army of the Cumberland paused to catch its breath after maneuvering Bragg's Confederate army completely out of Middle Tennessee.

The grind of eleven hard days in the saddle at least took John's mind off the predicament he'd gotten himself into: unofficially married to one woman, officially engaged to another. But the dilemma roared back into his awareness, spinning his mind with incompatible thoughts and emotions. Retrieving his prayer book, he sought comfort from Psalm 51.

> *Have mercy upon me, O God, according to thy lovingkindness: according unto the multitude of thy tender mercies blot out my transgressions.*
>
> *Wash me thoroughly from mine inequity, and cleanse me from my sin.*

***

Like John Lockridge, First Lieutenant Samuel L. Marshall was one of the rare men in the Western army who didn't come from a farming community. Chicago was his home.

And like the captain, Marshall was college educated, or at least he'd started on it. He'd withdrawn to volunteer for the army. About the only thing they didn't have in common was politics. Marshall's family were Democrats who'd backed Stephen Douglas for the senate against Lincoln and again two years later when the two squared off in the presidential election. But the Marshalls were "war Democrats," solidly behind the president's effort to preserve the Union. Looking beyond their political difference, the two young officers quickly developed a deepening friendship that served them well as the war ground on.

Crammed together in their dog tent at the end of their unrelenting rain-drenched march, John couldn't keep from spilling his story about Carrie to his close friend. But not the whole story.

At first John had thought that Carrie just intrigued him—her intelligence, her curiosity, her ambition for independence. He didn't know girls like that even existed. But when he noticed that thoughts of her filled most of his waking hours and saw how desperately he longed to be with her, John realized it was something more. She wouldn't at first glance strike anyone as particularly pretty, but she was to him, and he recalled feeling a bit of a stir when he saw her dressed up on Easter Sunday.

"I'd have to be blind and deaf, Lockridge, not to see what was happening," Marshall said. "What do you propose to do?"

John paused before trying to answer. "I'm thinking I need to go home. Straighten things out. Maybe there will be some furloughs like after Stones River now that we're in another lull."

"I don't pretend to know much about these matters, Lockridge, but I wonder if an attachment formed with a girl in these unrealistic circumstances is destined to last. When you do get home to Columbus, the old flame might reignite. Carrie could fade into distant memory."

"I've thought of that," said John, feeling a sharp pain in the pit of his stomach. Carrie could be carrying his child.

***

It took a while for the mail to catch up with the army, and when it did, John had three letters: one from his mother, one from Carrie, and one from Miranda. Guilt had driven him to resume writing her while the army was still at Murfreesboro. It was difficult, and deceitful to be sure, but he forced himself to correspond with her as if nothing had changed. Now though, away from Carrie, John was animated in his letter to Miranda, which surprised him. And worried him a little too. He put off writing Carrie until after he replied to Miranda and to his mother.

Decherd, Tenn.
July 10, '63

Dear Carrie,

The mail arrived today, and I was excited beyond words to receive yours. I've read it over so many times that Marshall says I'm ready for the asylum.

I feel like a prophet. I predicted Rosecrans would drive toward Manchester and try to get between Bragg and Chattanooga. That's exactly what we did. The plan was to get astride the railroad, cut the Rebs off from their line of supply and retreat, and make them turn and fight. The rain that began on June 24, the day we marched out of Murfreesboro, didn't let up for ten days, which slowed us, and the Johnnies managed to get away to Chattanooga.

We're camped now at a most beautiful spot only a mile or so from the foot of the Cumberland Mtn. These are the first real mountains I've ever laid eyes on. When we reached here on Independence Day, our brigade was ordered to follow the Rebs as they fled. We'd gone less than a mile along the forested plateau when we received orders to discontinue our pursuit and march back down the mountain. I've heard there are the beginnings of an Episcopal college on the mtn. and regret I didn't get to see it.

We're starting to get something to eat after going without for most of our march. I've become quite good at picking blackberries. But these Tennessee chiggers are something awful!

The rumors fly fast and furious about our next move. We'll head for the Tenn. River next, but after that, who knows? There's talk that we'll march toward Knoxville. Others say we'll go south to cut Bragg off from Atlanta. We hear our troops have fanned across North Alabama, and Athens and Decatur are in Union hands.

Tennessee Johnnies are deserting in droves. We brought several back from our foray up the mtn. They have no interest in keeping up the fight now that the Confederates have abandoned their state. The loss of Middle Tenn. is a bitter blow to the Confederacy. Word has reached us of a big battle in the East at a place called Gettysburg, but we don't know the outcome. And we've heard Vicksburg on the Miss. R. is on its last leg, surrounded by Grant's army.

Please write again soon. I'll do the same. Give my regards to your mother and Sarah, and say hello to Cassie and Sampson.

John stared blankly at the paper. How should he sign it? He couldn't decide, so he slid it into his valise and went about his duties. Just before mail call, he retrieved the letter. With a surge of jittery nervousness, he put his pen to the paper, fully aware that at this moment, maybe even more than their impromptu wedding and their intimate time together, he was marking his point of no return.

Your loving husband,
John

CHAPTER EIGHT

August 1863

John Lockridge wouldn't be going home to Columbus. Major General Rosecrans decreed that there would be no furloughs. And no ladies would be visiting the front like during the last interlude. Rosecrans needed everyone to focus on preparing for the next march.

The near bloodless campaign clearing Middle Tennessee of Confederates hadn't softened President Lincoln's obsession to liberate the Unionist majority in the eastern third of the state. "I do as much for East Tennessee as I would, or could, if my own home and family were in Knoxville," the president responded to a petition from Appalachian loyalists seeking relief from the iron fist of Confederate control.

The first week in August, General Bradley returned from a council of the army's brigade and division commanders with the news that Rosecrans had received an ultimatum from General Halleck in Washington. "Your forces must move forward without delay. You will daily report the movement of each corps 'til you cross the Tennessee River."

William S. Rosecrans wasn't anything if not stubborn. He planned on doing just as he'd done in Nashville in the fall and at Murfreesboro in the spring and early summer. He announced his intention to stay put until he was satisfied that his army was ready for the next move, replying to Washington that if he were not permitted the discretion to decide when to launch the next campaign, he should be relieved of command. The bluff worked. The Ohioan bought himself a little more time. But still, there would be no furloughs.

***

John decided it was time to come clean with Miranda even if he had to do it long distance. His conscience was gnawing on him so deeply that it was keeping him awake at night. So he took advantage of the army's brief inactivity to compose a letter. He'd have to be careful in the way he worded it. He couldn't sugarcoat the news to Miranda, yet the way he phrased it might determine how he'd be received when he returned home to Columbus. Bringing his new wife there to live after the war may not be an option, but he desperately wanted to avoid any estrangement from his own family. His mother's letter chastising him for neglecting his fiancée was still fresh in his mind.

The captain wasn't satisfied with his first letter, so he tried again. Then a third time. His mind still didn't rest easy, so he let his composition sit for a few days. When word came that the army was moving out, he retrieved the letter from his valise to date, sign, and mail. He read it again, but it still didn't seem right. So he tossed it on the campfire, resigned to continuing his disturbing double life a little longer.

***

The next stop for the Army of the Cumberland was the Tennessee River. It flows southwesterly through the Great Appalachian Valley from Knoxville to Chattanooga where it comes up against the eastern escarpment of the Cumberland Plateau. The river then twists around the northern point of Lookout Mountain, threads between several other mountains, and then continues southwesterly into Alabama. The river and the parallel mountains making up the Plateau presented formidable barriers to the Union army on its push into the heart of the Confederacy.

The Tennessee, it turned out, didn't present much of an obstacle at all. Only some scattered Rebel cavalry protected the opposite bank. The retreating Confederates had destroyed the Nashville & Chattanooga Railroad crossing at Bridgeport, so the army was forced to linger a few days while engineers set out pontoon bridges.

John took advantage of the short lull to write Carrie. He felt a tad queasy from her news. He was navigating uncharted waters.

Near Stevenson, Ala.
August 30, '63

Dearest Wife,

I received your news with a twinge of disappointment but also relief. It would complicate your life unmercifully now for you to be with child.

We left the Winchester area on Aug. 15 and followed the railroad over the mountain. We're camped on the bank of the Tennessee River in a little corner of Ala. the railroad runs through on its way to Chattanooga. It's a supremely beautiful spot. The river has cut a narrow valley between two towering mountains, the plateau we came over and Sand Mtn. in front of us. I'm told that beyond it is a deep valley and yet another mountain, Lookout.

There aren't many Johnnies around, just some disorganized cavalry. The bulk of the Rebel army is at Chattanooga. We should have an easy time crossing the Tennessee. Where we'll go once we cross is anybody's guess, but you can bet Old Rosey has something clever up his sleeve.

I'm intrigued by your proposal. I've never thought about living in Philadelphia or any big Eastern city. Are you sure there would be a position for you after the men return from the war? I've another idea for us. The

West. Yes, the West. The marriage we have in mind for ourselves will be easier if we're not so oppressed by the dictates of convention. From what I've read, the Colorado Territory is expected to boom after the war. There will be a need for teachers. And lawyers. Or maybe California? Or Oregon? It's now a state.

I suppose I'm putting the 'cart before the horse' but after Lee's defeat at Gettysburg, Grant's victory at Vicksburg, and our sweep of Middle Tenn., the Confederacy is near its end. All that remains is for us to land a knockout punch on Bragg.

I haven't had much opportunity to update my nature notebook. I did note that the mountains have lots of pine, something I didn't see around Murfreesboro. Plenty of cedar, but no pine. There seem to be two or three different kinds, but I don't know what they are. The river is lined with sycamore and silver maple. Turkey vultures soar below the mountain bluffs.

Duty calls. I must close. Longing for our reunion, I am.

Your husband,
John

CHAPTER NINE

September 1863

Like waves on the ocean, thought John Lockridge, standing on the east brow of Lookout Mountain. He'd never seen the sea, but the rows of parallel ridges and valleys stretching east to the horizon looked as he imagined it.

General Rosecrans's strategy of dividing his army and sending it off in different directions worked for him in Middle Tennessee, so he tried it again in Northwest Georgia. As before, his goal was to get astride the railroad and cut the Confederates off from their line of supply and retreat, only this time it was the line from Chattanooga to Atlanta.

Major General George H. Thomas, leader of the corps that included Bradley's brigade, counseled against the maneuver, but the commanding general overruled him. He sent McCook's Corps far to the south where his men were to pivot east, climb over Lookout Mountain, descend into the rows of ridges and valleys, and strike the Atlanta railroad south of Dalton. Rosecrans sent Crittenden's Corps in the opposite direction around Lookout's knife-edged point to threaten the Rebel army at Chattanooga. Thomas would keep his corps between the other two, and after getting over Lookout and its spur, Pigeon Mountain, block the road south from Chattanooga near Lafayette. Bragg would be trapped in a vise.

Among the several risks in Rosecrans's strategy, one was paramount. Bragg might figure out that elements of the Federal army were far apart, separated by some of the most inhospitable terrain in Eastern America, and be emboldened to try to pick them off one at a time.

***

"That can only mean one thing," said Brigadier General Bradley to his staff standing on a rocky outcrop atop Lookout Mountain. A massive cloud of dust lifted skyward beyond Pigeon Mountain in the vicinity of Lafayette, Georgia. "Only a large body of men could stir up that much dust. The Rebs have evacuated Chattanooga. This is exactly what General Thomas had warned against. Our corps may be facing an entire Rebel army."

***

Lookout Mtn, Ga.
Sept. 8, '63

My Dear Carrie,

I write by candlelight from the mountain extending from Chattanooga into Ga. and Ala. Our two-day climb up here was the most difficult march we've ever made, but the scenery is splendid. I took note of the thickets of laurel in the gorges. I'm sure it's a sight when it blooms in the spring. I'll bet the gorges have an abundance of trillium. There are many tall hemlocks.

We're overlooking a lush cove between here and a spur called Pigeon Mtn. As the sun set behind me tonight, I saw far in the distance the purple outline of the Blue Ridge Mtns. It was a magnificent sight. I'm getting to like mountains. I dream of returning to these parts someday with you by my side.

We hear from deserting Johnnies that Bragg is retreating to Rome and maybe even Atlanta to escape the vise we're putting him in. Let's hope that's true. If it's not, we could be in for a nasty fight.

I ache for you over the headmaster's decision to wait out the war in Ala., but I don't see that he had any choice. Our army blocks his path back to Tennessee. And it would be too dangerous to travel with the child. Your resourcefulness impresses me. Why not try to start your own school? Now that your church is free again, it would be a good place for it if you can get some furniture. You didn't say whether you'd take boys as well as girls. Whatever you decide, I'm behind you all the way. If you need funds, I might be able to spare a little.

The hour is late. I'll write again soon.

All my love,
John

***

McLemore's Cove, near Lafayette, Ga.
Sept. 18, '63

Dear Wife,

Our division has descended into the handsome cove formed by Lookout and its spur, Pigeon Mtn. Blooming flowers line the fence rows. I've identified black-eyed Susan, Queen Anne's lace, goldenrod, sunflower and a blue one I can't identify. It may be aster. It's a welcome relief to be off the mountain where there was hardly any water. From this cove flow the headwaters of a creek called "Chickamauga," which I'm told means "river of death" in some native tongue.

Our situation is precarious. Bragg's whole army may be lurking across Pigeon Mtn. while ours is badly divided. On top of that, we hear that two divisions from Lee's army under Longstreet are on their way from Virginia.

Gen. Negley's adjutant just delivered word that Rosecrans has called off his plan to cut the railroad to Atlanta and ordered McCook's Corps far to the south to close up on us. We'll then all march north to Chattanooga to join Crittenden's Corps. It will be a risky maneuver. Our army will be strung out for miles, and should the Rebs figure that out, we could be in for a fight. If we make it to Chattanooga, at least we'll have taken that place.

I've never been one to talk about such things, but I find that I can't keep from talking about you. Today Marshall asked that I give him at least one day off. He said that if he heard another word about your brilliant mind and turquoise eyes, he might borrow a bayonet from a private and run me through. I think he's jealous.

I'm encouraged by the happy tone of your latest letter. Worrying won't accomplish a thing. That's what you taught me, and I'm pleased you're able to live it.

With Burnside now in East Tennessee, the entire state is back in the Union. Surely the Confederate government knows it's over.

I'll write when we're safely in Chattanooga. Keep your spirits up. Longing to see you again, I am.

Your husband,
John

***

The surgeons had sawn off John's left leg just above the knee.

Drifting in and out of consciousness and alternatively freezing and burning up, he couldn't distinguish between reality and dreams. His mother. He saw her weeping over the loss of her son and longed to comfort her. His father. He heard him preaching his funeral. Will they even have one? His sisters. Would he reunite with them someday on the other side? Miranda. She'd at least be spared the pain of knowing of his betrayal. Carrie. The army would notify his family, but how would she find out?

An orderly came by with water and something to eat. John gulped down the water but couldn't force himself to bite into the hard biscuit. Or the spoiled bacon. He just wanted more water.

***

The most urgent task facing the Union army after fleeing the field at Chickamauga was protecting itself in Chattanooga. Six miles of fortifications were built around two sides of the town while the Tennessee River guarded the other two. But Bragg's Confederates didn't pursue. Instead, they occupied the heights surrounding the town, Lookout Mountain and Missionary Ridge, intent on starving Rosecrans's army into submission.

It took a few days for the Federal army to settle in, and when it did, officers began drafting their battle reports. First Lieutenant Marshall, now the acting adjutant for Bradley's Brigade, collected casualty reports from the regiments for the brigadier's report to division headquarters. Of the 1,226 enlisted men in the brigade, nineteen had been killed, 173 wounded, and another 104 were missing, presumably captured. Of the 105 officers who saw action, one had lost his life, six were missing, and fourteen were wounded, and that included Captain Lockridge.

The brigade came out of the two days of fighting better than many. The Battle of Chickamauga produced 34,624 casualties on both sides, and as it would turn out, this was more than any battle in the war, save the three days at Gettysburg.

***

Sam Marshall hadn't conceived that he'd share such an intimacy with another man, but he felt a connection to John Lockridge closer even than with his own brother. Their growing up years were in some ways similar, but in other ways quite different. As best Sam could tell from their acquaintanceship of nine months, John's family lived the austere life one would expect for a clergyman. Sam's family wasn't afraid to show off their wealth. Their imposing mansion on Chicago's north side was crawling with Irish servants catering to their every need, and though Sam didn't share his parents' view, they considered their help much the same way wealthy Southerners considered their bonded, black house servants.

It was precisely his egalitarian point of view that got Sam shipped up to Evanston to the new Methodist college they were calling Northwestern. He'd started keeping company with an Irish girl his age, Pamela O'Neil, a teacher's assistant at one of the Catholic schools. She was the sister of the errand boy at his father's shipping business Sam had met at a dance the errand boy talked him into attending. Pamela was a vivacious, slightly plump girl who shared his love for reading and learning. He was completely at ease around her, and she seemed to be around him. Sam concealed the relationship from his family as best he could, knowing they'd disapprove, but inevitably word of it seeped home.

So in his nineteenth year, Sam became a college student. That life proved to be as short-lived as his romance with Pamela O'Neil, for at the end of his first year, in June 1861, Sam joined the throng of patriotic young men volunteering for the army. He agreed with President Lincoln: the rebellion of the Southern states had to be put down.

Being with Pamela had given Sam enough of a taste of affection to understand, if only a little, how his friend Lockridge could be so taken with the Tennessee girl. Carrie sounded a tad on the serious side for his own tastes, but then, Lockridge tilted to the serious side too.

Sam wondered how his friend was going to extricate himself from the predicament he'd gotten himself into with the two women. They'd discussed it briefly, but Sam had little to offer except to say: "Follow your heart. Don't let someone else's view of what's proper dictate your behavior."

***

It took some searching through the detritus that was now the Army of the Cumberland, but Sam located his friend in a large brick building not far from the Chattanooga depot. Hospital Seven, it was called, one of two set aside for officers. But labeling it a hospital was a stretch. Many of the seven thousand wounded overflowing Chattanooga went untreated. Half the army's surgeons were in Confederate custody, having remained on the field to tend to the wounded left behind. There were no beds and only a few cots. At least the men lying on the cold floor had blankets.

"Help me up, Marshall, I need to piss."

The lieutenant helped John stand on his wobbly right leg.

"Set the pot down. The colored orderlies empty them."

Sam helped him back down and sat beside him.

"I hate for you to see me like this," John said.

"I'm just glad to find you alive."

"What happened? What went wrong? How did I wind up in this filthy place?" John didn't recall much of anything after they'd marched north out of McLemore's Cove on September 18.

***

Thanks to the incompetence and even insubordination of his generals, Confederate commander Braxton Bragg had been thwarted in his plans to pick off one at a time the strung-out parts of the Federal army. When his quarrelsome generals had finally gotten around to launching an attack, Thomas's corps had dug in on the north end of the Federal column struggling toward Chattanooga on September 19.

The next day, Longstreet's newly arrived Easterners charged through an inadvertent breach in the Federal line, slicing it in two. Major General Rosecrans came unglued. Taking much of the Union army with him, the commander fled in panic to Chattanooga, leaving George H. Thomas the senior officer in the field. Brigadier General Charles Bradley's regiments had scattered in the chaos. But he wasn't one to retreat, so he and his staff fought their way to General Thomas's headquarters on Snodgrass Hill to make themselves useful.

Thomas wasn't sure how long the remnant of the army could hold out against the relentless Rebel assaults. He hoped the rising cloud of dust off toward Chattanooga was from Granger's Federal reserve corps marching to his aid, and not from Confederate reinforcements. He needed to know. Someone had to ride north to find out.

John Lockridge had mounted his horse, trotted off the hill, and followed a route west of the Lafayette Road in the direction of the rising dust. After running the gauntlet of sporadic fire from Forrest's dismounted Rebel cavalry, the captain spotted the stars and stripes fluttering on the vanguard of the column moving toward him. He turned to gallop back to General Thomas with the good news.

John couldn't tell at first what had happened. With Thomas's headquarters now in his view on the hill ahead, his vision grew dimmer and dimmer. The ground was littered with dying men, and their ghastly cries for help got fainter and fainter. Only when he pulled up to deliver the message was he aware of the cause of his light-headedness. One of Forrest's sharpshooters had found his mark.

"Put him on that wagon," ordered First Lieutenant Sam Marshall. "I'll get the word to General Thomas." Two privates had struggled to get John off his panting mare and onto a wagon tightly packed with bloody men of all ranks.

They were jostled the ten miles to Chattanooga, at least the ones who made it alive. The bodies of those who didn't were cast onto the side of the road.

***

"Sounds like we're lucky our whole army wasn't wiped out," said John after Sam told him the story.

"We are indeed." Sam looked around to insure that they couldn't be overheard and then leaned into John's ear. "I have it on good authority that the secretary of war has decided to remove Rosecrans."

"That shouldn't be a surprise, given what you've told me. When?"

"No one knows. Apparently the president wants to delay it."

"I hope Thomas replaces him."

"We all do. He saved the army from annihilation. They're calling him 'the Rock of Chickamauga.'"

"*Let us make a joyful noise to the rock of our salvation.* Psalm Ninety-Five," said John.

"I'll have to take your word for that. Anyway, it looks like we're in for a siege. The Johnnies didn't press us after the battle, but they command the heights, and it's next to impossible to get in and out of this miserable place. Chattanooga is surrounded by mountains and ridges."

"When I'm recovered enough to travel, they're supposed to send me to Nashville, but I guess it won't be anytime soon."

"At least not until Hooker reaches us."

Some fifteen thousand troops from the Army of the Potomac under Major General Joseph Hooker were making the circuitous rail journey from Virginia to rescue the trapped Army of the Cumberland. And William T. Sherman and his army were on the way from Mississippi. The only question was how long the surrounded Federals could hold out. The men had already been reduced to half rations, and there was talk that they'd soon be reduced to quarter rations. With little or nothing to eat, horses and mules were dying by the hundreds. The stench was unbearable, worse even than the hunger.

CHAPTER TEN

October 1863

A few days had gone by since Sam Marshall visited John. General Bradley had been to see him in the intervening days, and not just to check in on his adjutant whom he'd grown attached to. The brigadier wanted to personally give John the news; he was naming Marshall the new brigade adjutant and recommending him for promotion to captain.

The sickening odor of death that had greeted Sam when he first visited John was even worse this day. Isolated as they were in Chattanooga, there wasn't much the army could do for Chickamauga's wounded, and an increasing number of men's bodies were wearing out from lack of food. The foul odor of flesh rotting from gangrene mixed with the results of the widespread diarrhea and ceaseless vomiting, and it was all Sam could do to keep from being sick himself.

John was now on a cot at least, and the soon-to-be captain felt a stab of apprehension approaching it. The unease didn't stem so much from fear over how his friend was taking the news that he'd been replaced as it did from how he was handling the finality of it. The war was over for him. The life he'd known for twenty-five years was over too. He'd adjust; he wouldn't have any choice, but it would take time.

At least, Sam thought, Lockridge is capable of earning a living with his wits. He'll make out better than most men with missing limbs.

John seemed to be asleep. After staring down at him for a moment, Sam turned to leave.

"Don't go, Marshall."

The captain's voice was weak, and as quickly as Sam looked at him, John seemed to drift off again. Sam stayed put.

"I'm afraid, Marshall." John labored to speak. His eyes remained closed. "For the first time I'm afraid."

Sam took John's hand and held it as if he were a child. "You'll pull through, Lockridge, I'm certain of it. Men a lot worse off than you have made it."

Turning to face Sam, John opened his eyes. "It's not that. It's about her."

"Carrie?"

"Yes," he said, sighing, "Carrie. I'm afraid."

"Afraid of what?"

"That she won't want me anymore."

***

The hospital reeked even worse the next day, but Sam Marshall was relieved to find John much improved. The circuitous mountain route to the railhead at Bridgeport permitted a dribble of rations and supplies to reach Chattanooga, and the captain had managed to get his hands on a Nashville newspaper. He was sitting up reading it.

John put it aside as Sam sat on the cot.

"What's it like around here?" John asked.

"Hooker's divisions have reached Bridgeport, so it's only a matter of days 'til you'll be on your way to Nashville."

"I read in this paper that Crittenden and McCook have been sacked," John said. "Is that true?"

"It looks like it. That leaves Thomas as the only remaining corps commander. And our division commander has been sacked as well."

"Negley's gone too?"

"There are those urging his court-martial for abandoning the field, but Rosey took pity on him—gave him a medical leave to go home."

"What about him? Rosecrans."

"Word is that Lincoln's about to put Grant in command of all Western forces. It'll be up to him."

"I've always heard Grant's not high on Thomas."

"He supposedly thinks even less of Rosecrans. They served together in Mississippi, you know. Regardless of what Grant thinks of Thomas, everyone expects him to give Thomas command of our army."

"Well let's hope so."

They were both quiet, absorbing the consequences of the news. If it could be called news. Rumors and news were impossible to differentiate.

"Marshall, I need you to do something for me."

"Anything you ask, Lockridge."

"My trunk, you'll have to find my trunk. In it should be my leather valise. Please bring it to me."

"That shouldn't be too difficult."

"And, Marshall, if they move me before you get back, please hang on to it. Don't let anything happen to it. We'll meet up again some day."

"I give you my word, Lockridge."

***

Sam found the captain's trunk, but it had taken longer than he anticipated, so it was a few days before he made it back to the squalid warehouse crammed full of sick and wounded officers.

"Here's your little grip."

"Oh, thank you so much. Help me up, will you? I've had a bit of a setback."

Sam slid his arms under John's shoulders and pulled him to a sitting position.

"Thanks."

The captain took the valise and pulled out a drawing of some sort. His eyes filled with tears.

"A trillium," John said. "A flower. Everything's in threes." He held it up for Sam to see. "Sort of like me now."

John shoved it back into the valise and removed paper, pen, and ink.

"I need to write some letters." He laid the valise on his lap as he would a portable writing table and began writing. It was a struggle, Sam noticed. John didn't write much before he folded the paper and stuffed it into an envelope.

"To my family, letting them know I survived."

"Would you like me to address it for you?" Sam asked.

"That would be nice."

"You're going to write Carrie, I assume."

"My next letter."

"Would you like me to take it down for you?"

"That's asking too much."

"If you don't mind me saying so, Lockridge, you're going to have to get used to letting people do things for you, for a little while anyway."

"It's not easy to accept. I'm embarrassed."

"I'm happy to do the letter."

"Thanks. It won't be long."

Sam knelt down, took the pen and ink, and used the valise as his writing surface.

Chattanooga
Oct. 8, '63

Dear Carrie,

I said I'd write from Chattanooga but didn't think it would take so long. I'm sure you've heard of the big battle near here. I've sustained a grievous wound, but I'll be all right. (Marshall is taking down the letter.)

They're shipping me to a Nashville hospital as soon as the line opens. It shouldn't be much longer. Perhaps Miss Forbes can look in on me. I hope you can visit. If Ma is able to come, you'll get to meet her.

John took a deep breath.

"Is that it?" Sam asked.

"I'll write myself when I feel stronger, in a day or two."

"Here, Lockridge, sign it."

***

Sam returned two days later with John's leather valise tucked under his left arm. Inside it was a letter from Carrie that had just arrived. Sam had stuffed the letter unopened into the valise. When he approached the cot, the man rolled over and looked up at him. But it wasn't John.

"Where's Lockridge?"

The man closed his eyes and rolled back over.

Sam grabbed an orderly. "Where'd they take the other officer who was in that bed?"

"I don't know for sure, sir. They've moved some north of the river."

"Well, who does know?"

"The surgeon, sir. You'll have to ask the surgeon."

Sam scurried up the row of cots until he reached the end, but he saw no surgeon. He went in the other direction and found one.

"Doctor, my friend Lockridge, he was on that cot over there," said Sam, pointing. "Where have you taken him?"

"The captain on General Bradley's staff?"

"Yes, him. Where is he?"

"I'm sorry, Lieutenant."

"Sorry, sorry about what?"

"He had a setback."

"Where is he?"

"He didn't make it through the night."

CHAPTER ELEVEN

June 1868

It was in the third year after the end of the war and cool for a June night. Carrie was soaked to the bone. She tried to sleep, but every time she dozed off she was awakened by her own shivering. The hour was late, well past midnight, and she still had four hours to wait for her train back to Murfreesboro.

"Here lady, take this."

She looked up from the waiting room bench to see the Chattanooga stationmaster standing over her with a wool blanket.

"I keep these on hand. Hardly a day goes by now without one of you Northern ladies spending the night here."

"That's kind of you." She unfolded the blanket and wrapped it around herself.

Northern lady. Hardly, but she kept the truth to herself. It really doesn't matter, she thought. North, South, alone or with family, we're all seeking the same thing: finality and closure.

***

More than once in the past three years Carrie had recalled her friend Lizzy Schultz's comparison of being a teacher and living at the school to being an indentured servant. Carrie lived in a little room at the school where she taught in Nashville. The students were eager and inquisitive, and she loved teaching the girls. The school's proprietors treated her kindly, but Carrie's life was constricted. She barely had time for worship and the women's activities at Christ Church, the one she'd attended years earlier when she was a student in Nashville. She found time for only a scrap of a social life. So when she saw the newspaper article about the new national cemetery in Chattanooga, Carrie couldn't permit herself the luxury of even thinking about visiting it.

She'd saved the article, though. Rereading it when she was back at her mother's after school let out for the year, she contemplated going. She had no clue what she'd find, but the more she thought about it, the more she wanted to make the trip. Her mother suggested that it would be best if all three of them went, but Carrie resisted. She appreciated the offer, but she wanted to go alone. She didn't want any distractions.

Lookout Mountain attained prominence in the weeks following word of John's passing when it was the scene of the first of the three days' fighting that freed the Federal army from the grip of the Confederate siege. Carrie was eager to see the mountain, but as the train looped around its point headed into Chattanooga, all she saw was the wall of green disappearing into the clouds. There was a cool mist, more like winter weather than early summer.

A steady flow of visitors needed transportation from the Chattanooga depot, and hack drivers congregated there whenever a train was scheduled to arrive from the north. The drivers had learned the cemetery's layout, and as part of the fare they assisted their customers in locating loved ones' graves.

Those who'd lost their lives at Chickamauga were the first to be reinterred at the new cemetery, and Carrie's driver led her to the oldest graves. After paying the man, she instructed him not to wait for her.

"Ma'am, it's a two-mile walk back in this drizzle."

"Thank you for your concern," she replied, "but I'd just as soon walk back."

He left her beside concentric semicircles of headstones watched over by a newly planted oak. After he rattled across the railroad tracks headed back to town, Carrie inhaled deeply and began her search. She treaded across the soggy turf painstakingly reading the names on each of the marble headstones. She completed the first row and moved to the second. The heat rose in her cheeks and her chest thumped as she stepped from headstone to headstone.

For some reason that made no sense, she was surprised when she came to it. Perhaps deep down she didn't want to find it.

She fell to her knees. There were no tears; only the drizzle of the rain.

It's unfair, she said to herself, his life compressed into just three words.

John Lockridge
Ohio

CHAPTER TWELVE

June 1875

Ten years after he'd come home from the war, Sam Marshall sat alone in a second floor room of his family's home a few blocks off Lake Michigan in Evanston. Tucked in the inside pocket of his wool suit coat was the one document indispensable for his trip: the letter from the bank president in Sacramento offering him a position. Later that day he would load his bags and himself into his father's elegant, two-horse carriage and be chauffeured to the depot down in Chicago.

His parents had hosted a farewell reception for him the night before, where family, friends, and other bank employees dropped by to say goodbye and wish him well. Alone with his thoughts in the empty room, Sam visualized the face of every one of them. They were the most important people in his life. He felt a lump in his throat with the awareness that he wouldn't be around to witness the school graduations, weddings, and other milestones in the lives of his nieces and nephews.

I'll miss them the most, he thought. But I need to start a new life.

On the surface it didn't look that way. He'd returned from the war to complete his studies at Northwestern and landed a coveted spot at one of Chicago's leading institutions. His steady rise through the ranks generated speculation that one day he'd head the bank. Considered one of the city's most eligible bachelors, Sam was in demand on Chicago's high-end social circuit, but his inability to form an attachment with any of the several young women who'd be pleased to have him for a husband was symptomatic of the deeper disorder in his life.

He had trouble sitting still now and found it increasingly difficult to concentrate. On nights when he was finally able to sleep, visions of the unspeakable horrors of the war invaded his dreams. His temper grew shorter by the day, and he'd turned to drinking more than he should. Sam couldn't name his malady, but whatever it was, he wasn't the person he used to be. Or wanted to be.

The fire that had consumed much of Chicago—and prompted his parents to build their fine house out in Evanston—had pushed Sam over the edge. He spent a little more than a year investigating alternatives before he decided California was the place for a new life.

He wasn't going to be taking the leather valise that rested on the low table in front of him. He'd been faithful to his pledge to his friend John Lockridge, even though he'd never see him again, at least not in this life. The valise stayed in Sam's baggage when the Union army fought its way out of Chattanooga in the month following John's passing and was with Sam in 1864 when they skirmished their way to Atlanta. Sam took the little grip with him as Sherman wrecked his way to Savannah, then through the Carolinas in 1865, and finally home later that year.

What should I do with it now, he pondered. He'd never once, in all those years, studied the contents. But he'd opened it twice, once to stuff inside it Carrie's letter to deliver to Lockridge that awful long-ago day when he discovered John had passed in the night and again to put away her letter thanking him for the news about John's death.

Sam reached into the valise, and pulled out the first paper his hand touched. It was Carrie's letter to him. He was struck even now as he was back then by its brevity.

Murfreesboro
Oct. 16, '63

My Dear Lieutenant,

It was kind of you to send word of John's passing. My heart had told me something was wrong. He treasured your friendship. May God protect you from harm.

Respectfully,
Carrie Blaylock

Sam pulled out another paper. It was the unopened letter she'd written to John after Chickamauga, the one Lockridge never saw. So sad, so miserably sad, thought Sam. Like thousands of other letters written by loved ones unaware that their boys were dead or dying.

He set aside the unopened letter and reached into the valise again, this time pulling out a stack of ten or so letters tied together with a ribbon. Lockridge had arranged Carrie's letters chronologically, the oldest dated the day the army had marched out of Murfreesboro. Just like Lockridge, Sam thought, always so damned organized. The last of the opened letters in the bundle bore the date of September 5, 1863.

Let me think, Sam said to himself. That was about the time we crossed the Tennessee River and began crawling over those God-awful mountains. The bundle contained ten to twelve of Carrie's letters.

Next he tugged out a pencil drawing, of what he couldn't tell at first, but saw that it was the flower with three petals and three leaves. Turning it over, he saw that John had written something on the back. Sam squinted to read it. *Trillium. April 1863. She drew this for me.*

Sam reached into his vest for his watch. "Two more hours; I hate this waiting to leave," he said. After sitting for a minute or two, he picked up Carrie's unopened letter, the one

John never saw. It didn't seem right that it should never be read.

M'boro
Sept 25, '63

Dearest John,

My hand trembles. Word has reached us of the massive battle along the Chickamauga. I fear that harm has befallen you. I try to tell myself that it's more likely you are unhurt, but my anxiety is unyielding.

Words fail me as I try to put on paper the depth of my gratitude to God for sending you to me. I've never felt as safe and secure as when I'm in your arms. I've never been so comfortable being a woman as when I'm with you. No one has ever made me feel so capable and so strong. My only hope is that you'll return to me.

The setback for your army does not bode well for a quick end to the war. It gets more difficult each chore-filled day to stay here and wait. Mother says it wouldn't be acceptable for me to help the Methodists with their colored school here. Nashville is a more realistic option. I hear from Lizzy that a Mr. and Mrs. Ward are talking about opening a new school for girls there. It will be rigorous, not just for show. I've decided to go back to Nashville to investigate it. I'm not sure when, but it will be after the weather cools some.

Speaking of Lizzy, the influx of wounded from the battle prohibits Gunter from getting a furlough. They won't be visiting Cincinnati anytime soon, and Gunter is committed to her meeting his son before they marry. Lizzy frets over whether the boy will like her and fears he may 'veto' the marriage. I'll bet by the end of their first day together he'll be curled on her lap as she reads to him. She worries too much. (I'm one to talk!)

Sarah continues her probing questions. She's drawn to you, as I'm sure you know, and she'd be pleased with our news, I think. But she's still a girl, and I fear that she might let it slip. I can't take that chance. At times it feels deceitful not to let my very sister in on our secret. But you know what it would do to my life if word got out. And, of course, I haven't told Mother.

You mentioned the West. Would I want to live in such a rough-and-tumble place? It would be measurably better than the way I live now, I suppose. I'm open to anyplace where we won't be choked by convention. Just get back to me!

John, we don't know what the future holds, but of one thing I'm certain. I'll never in all my life have but one husband, of that you can rest assured.

Please, John, write if you can.

All my love,
your wife.

"What?" Sam said. He read it again: *your wife*. "Husband? Wife?" Obviously something had happened, something Lockridge never shared with him. Sam picked up the stack of remaining letters. He untied the ribbon and opened the first one, the one she'd written the day the army marched out of Murfreesboro.

M'boro
June 24, '63

Dearest John,

I write at the end of the day because only now am I calm enough. I awoke this morning to the sound of your army on the move. I regret that we were prohibited from saying a proper goodbye.

As soon as I dressed, I dashed to the pike and was fortunate to find an officer who told me the whole army was marching away from Murfreesboro for good, except for a division being left behind. Where to he didn't know, but he was under the impression that his division, Sheridan's, was marching toward Bell Buckle and that Thos. Corps was marching toward Manchester. There will be another horrid battle, and I fear for your safety. I'll try to have faith that you'll return to me.

I awoke Monday morning dreaming of you lying next to me, my husband of one day. Oh that I should be so fortunate! Some day, I pray, and hope you feel the same. No, I trust you do feel the same.

Mother sends her regards. I have not shared our secret with her, but of course, it may soon become obvious. Only time will tell.

The rain is pounding now, and I can't stand the thought of you out in it, unprotected. But I suppose I'd better get used to it.

I have no idea where this letter will find you, but I pray it finds you safe and well. "The Lord shall preserve thee from all evil: he shall preserve thy soul." Psalm 121.

Write to me John.

With all my love,
Carrie

One by one, in chronological order just the way Lockridge had saved them, Sam read Carrie's letters. His emotions swelled with each one. At first he thought it was just sadness for them, for their loss, but then he realized he was sad for himself too, for never having experienced a love like John and Carrie shared. He'd sought out Pamela when he returned in 1865, only to find that she'd died in childbirth the year before while her husband was away in the army.

Whatever happened to Carrie? Sam felt like he'd known her, Lockridge talked about her so much. In her letters she appeared as intelligent and thoughtful as Lockridge insisted she was. She seemed to be aiming for teaching in Nashville. Did she? Did that headmaster John mentioned a few times return after the war and try to court her? What became of her pretty sister? And her mother who Lockridge so admired? Sam's nerves were already on edge even before reading the letters, and he slumped back into his chair, shaky and drained.

What should he do with the letters? Leave them around for someone to paw through? That didn't seem right. They were intimate and private. Throw them into the trash? That didn't seem right either. No, I'll burn them. And I'll give the valise to one of the Irish servants. The driver, his boy can use it for school. Sam gathered the letters in a pile and took them downstairs with him to leave for the depot. Detouring to the kitchen, he stood looking at the fire their cook had going inside the claw-footed iron stove. He hesitated. It seemed so final, like the loss of a life. In a sense it was, his final goodbye to his friend Lockridge.

He opened the door to the fire box, and slowly set inside each piece of paper, one at a time. He stared at the fire until the last one turned to ash. But he kept the drawing of the flower. The trillium.

The ride to the depot seemed to take forever. His mind churned with anxiety over the trip to California, sadness over leaving his family and friends, and hope for a new life. And the letters, Carrie's letters. He couldn't get them out of his mind.

Sam insisted that no one go along to the Chicago depot, and after bidding farewell to Kevin, the driver, he lugged his bags into the station house to start the first leg of his trip. He would stay with friends in Omaha for a few days before boarding the Union Pacific, the eastern end of the new Pacific railroad. There would be stops along the way in new places like Cheyenne and Reno, and if all went as planned, he'd be in Sacramento in ten days at the latest.

Sam stalled on his way to the ticket window. He couldn't purge from his mind the suspicion that this move to California was a mistake, a futile attempt to change himself by changing his surroundings. But I can't go back, he thought. It would be too humiliating. He stood amidst the throng of humanity pressing around him, trying to collect himself, and then pushed his way on to the ticket window.

"Where to, mister?"

"How do I get to Nashville, Tennessee?"

AUTHOR'S NOTE

The Union's Army of the Cumberland's stay at Murfreesboro, Tennessee, in 1863 was one of the longest an entire Federal army remained in one place in the South. While digging into that period for other writing projects, I wondered about relationships between the occupiers and the occupied. Also, I've always been curious about the impact on women who witnessed the unspeakable horror of a major battle and who suffered through unimaginable deprivation. My then nineteen-year-old great grandmother was among the local women who waded into the carnage after the Battle of Chickamauga to care for the wounded.

I studied a long list of scholarly works, the most helpful of which were *When the Yankees Came: Conflict & Chaos in the Occupied South, 1861-1865* by Stephen V. Ash; *Mothers of Invention: Women of the Slaveholding South in the American Civil War* by Drew Gilpin Faust; *Confederate Daughters: Coming of Age during the Civil War* by Victoria E. Ott; and my late friend and mentor Walter Durham's two volumes, *Nashville The Occupied City: The First Seventeen Months February 16, 1862, to June 30, 1863* and *Reluctant Partners: Nashville and the Union, July 1, 1863 to June 30, 1865.*

Two eminent historians, Carol Bucy and Antoinette Van Zelm, both authorities on women in the Civil War, helped me get started on this project by answering my questions and by pointing me to primary sources.

I examined nearly fifty published and unpublished diaries written by Southern women during the war. The two most influential were the diaries of Sarah Morgan and Eliza Francis Andrews. The most recently published edition of Morgan's is *Sarah Morgan: The Civil War Diary of a Southern Woman* edited by Charles East, and Andrews's latest is *Wartime Journal of a Georgia Girl: 1864-1865.* Andrews's post-war memoir, *Journal of a Georgia Woman: 1870-1872,* was enlightening as well. Unlike many diarists about whom little is known after the war, the two of them went on to become successful writers and left paper trails documenting their fascinating and unconventional lives right up to their deaths, Morgan in 1909 and Andrews in 1931.

Some of Sarah Morgan's post-war writings can be found in *The Correspondence of Sarah Morgan and Francis Warrington Dawson with Selected Editorials Written by Sarah Morgan for the Charleston News and Courier,* edited by Giselle Roberts, published by the University of Georgia in 2004. Morgan is an integral part of the 2011 book, *Upheaval in Charleston: Earthquake and Murder on the Eve of Jim Crow* by Susan Millar Williams and Stephen G. Hoffius. The murder referred to in the title is that of Morgan's newspaper editor-husband. Andrews's best-selling 1876 novel set during the Civil War, *A Family Secret,* reissued in 2005, offers a glimpse into life during those turbulent times.

One unpublished diary that I studied has since been published, *The Diary of Nannie Haskins Williams: A Southern Woman's Story of Rebellion and Reconstruction, 1863-1890*, edited by Minoa D. Uffelman, Ellen Kanervo, Eleanor Williams, and Phyllis Smith. Another diary I studied was in 2014 republished as a biography by Carolyn Newton Curry, *Suffer & Grow Strong: The Life of Ella Gertrude Clanton Thomas, 1834-1907.* Dr. Curry's book is essential reading for anyone interested in how the Civil War transformed the lives of Southern women, for Gertrude Thomas evolved from a slaveholding plantation owner to a leading advocate for women's suffrage. A diary published while I was working on this novel, *In the Shadow of the Enemy: The Civil War Journal of Ida Powell Dulany,* is superbly written and expertly edited by

Mary L. Mackall, Steven F. Meserve, and Anne Mackall Sasscer. I was asked to review it for *H-Net*, the online humanities and social studies journal. Other diaries have been published in periodicals such as the *Tennessee Historical Quarterly*.

I pored over unpublished diaries at the Tennessee State Library and Archives, the David M. Rubenstein Rare Book and Manuscript Library at Duke University, and the Southern Historical Collection at the University of North Carolina. Sarah Morgan's papers, including her original Civil War diary, are at Duke. The staffs at those collections were quite helpful.

I turned to several sources to learn more about the day-to-day experiences of Union soldiers in Middle Tennessee during the period covered in the novel. The two most helpful were *Memoirs of a Volunteer* by John Beatty and *Three Years in the Army of the Cumberland* by James Connolly, edited by Paul M. Angle. As the title suggests, Brigadier General Beatty's is a memoir; Major Connolly's account is in the form of detailed letters to his new wife back in Illinois. Good background reading for the Union side is *Days of Glory: The Army of the Cumberland, 1861-1865* by Larry J. Daniel.

To refresh my recollection about the two major battles that bookend the story, I returned to Peter Cozzens's *No Better Place to Die,* about Stones River near Murfreesboro, December 31, 1862-January 2, 1863, and *This Terrible Sound,* about Chickamauga near Chattanooga, September 19 & 20, 1863.

***

Though the book is fiction, the historical facts are accurate with a few exceptions. The Episcopal church in Murfreesboro wasn't established until after the Civil War. The Murfreesboro cemetery Carrie visited was established in 1888. And Nashville's Church Street appears on most maps of the day as "Spring Street," though there are a few wartime references to it as Church Street.

ABOUT THE AUTHOR

Robert Brandt is the author of books and articles on Tennessee history, travel, and outdoors. His articles have appeared in *Sierra, Tennessee Historical Quarterly, and Tennessee Conservationist.* His contributions to the *Tennessee Encyclopedia of History and Culture* include entries about the period covered in the story. He is a retired judge and lawyer living in Nashville with his wife, Anne. This is his first work of fiction.